Treacle Town

Brian Conaghan

ANDERSEN PRESS

First published in 2023 by
Andersen Press Limited
20 Vauxhall Bridge Road, London SW1V 2SA, UK
Vijverlaan 48, 3062 HL Rotterdam, Nederland
www.andersenpress.co.uk

2 4 6 8 10 9 7 5 3 1

British Library Cataloguing in Publication Data available.

ISBN 978 1 83913 361 9

Printed and bound in Great Britain by Clays Ltd, Elcograf S.p.A.

About the Author

Brian Conaghan's young adult and middle-grade novels have been published in a variety of languages. His 2014 book, *When Mr Dog Bites* was shortlisted for the Carnegie Medal, while *The Bombs That Brought Us Together* (2016) won the Costa Children's Book Award. *The Weight of a Thousand Feathers* (2018) won the An Post Irish Teen Book of the Year as well as the Children's Books Ireland honour award. To date, his middle-grade novels, *Cardboard Cowboys* and *Swimming on the Moon* (2021, 2023) have been nominated and shortlisted for a slew of awards.

Brian's work is primarily focussed on the lives and relationships of working-class teens, and those characters who live in the margins of society. *Treacle Town* continues in this vein, but is the first of his novels to be set in his hometown of Coatbridge; giving him first-hand knowledge and experience of the lives lived within the book.

Before becoming a full-time writer, Brian worked as an English, Theatre Studies and Classics secondary school teacher in Scotland, Italy and Ireland. After twenty-one years of work and travel, Brian currently lives back in his native Coatbridge.

Biscuit

It takes three people to hold up Biscuit's mum. Poor woman's bawling her pipes out; squealing like a banshee, so she is. Hits you deep in the pit. It's hard not to look, but every time I do, Biscuit's big sister Denise fires hate-hissing daggers my way. Rotten to the core that one, always said it. I glance at Wee Z, Trig and Nails cos they've been getting daggers too. My face is probably as ashen as theirs. Grey with guilt. Or just lost in the loss. Truth? I want to bawl like Biscuit's mum. No joke, feels as if my throat's gonna explode from my neck and splatter all over the altar. I do a silent scream, which I seem to have mastered over the years.

The sight and sound of this scene would shatter anyone's heart. That noise of death stokes memories. Nightmare stuff; loathe it, that noise.

Tell you one thing for nothing, there's two ways I'm turning on the waterworks in front of all these people: none and fuck all. Imagine the slagging afterwards?

'That's my boy in there,' Biscuit's mum keeps screaming. *That's my laddie in there.*

1

That's my laddie.
Until it fades into:
My laddie.
My.
Laddie.
Before ending with a murmur of: *My wee boy.*

Her howls echo right through the chapel; makes you fear for the stained glass.

Biscuit, my mate. Our mucker. One of the troops. In there. Lying in his crisp shirt and tie like some posh waiter. Not as much as a scratch on his chops. Zero hint of carnage. Peaceful. Adorable. A proverbial angel. He'd probably have preferred to be in his North Face trackie right enough. He loved that thing. Mint, so it was. Didn't tell him that though. Should've. Eighteenth birthday present. I got him a bottle of Mad Dog. *Mad Dog for a mad dog,* I told him.

We first saw the angel in him when we went round to his gaff for the prayers. Special invite from his mum. You had to squeeze sideways to get through to where he was; think the whole town was belting out the rosary that night. As soon as we made it to the living room, it was game over. Nobody told us the lid would be open, and him lying there as if it was siesta time. I just thought everyone would be sitting around sobbing, sipping tea and munching the odd triangle sandwich. Well, they were actually, but … the lid. Fuck me, some shock that was, I'm telling you. But, what

2

could we do? No option to bolt, same door in, same door out. So, like every other awkward person, we queued for our final gander.

I'm standing there, peering in at my pal, and Wee Z kept tugging at me; thought he was gonna rip my new Berghaus jacket to bits. Ordinarily you'd get a sore jaw just for the thought. Trig and Nails shuffled and sniffed behind.

I clutched the side of the coffin for dear life, it's practically holding me up, and I notice that all his freckles are gone. How? I placed four fingers on his forehead. Dead gentle like. All I wanted to do was bend down and give him a wee kiss on the cheek; whisper something like, *I'll miss you forever, ya zoomer*, but for some reason I couldn't do it; too scared in case I wouldn't be able to get off him again, pulled the whole thing to the floor, two of us rolling around on the rug. One last hurrah. I put the back of my hand against his cheek, and, in my head, said, *Sleep well, Biscuit. Love ye, son. Always have. Always will.* Then I slunk away to let the others have their go. Mrs McVitie was sunk on a chair. Zombie-esque. I was shittin' it. Didn't want to speak to her but there was no escape, you had to pass when waddling away from the coffin. It was an unofficial one-way system in his living room. Some woman was beside her, sitting on the arm, rubbing her shoulders. I didn't want to look at Mrs McVitie, or spout the usual shite people say. My face was matted with guilt. Legs felt like liquid. She must've known I was heart sorry. She must've. How could she not? Beyond sorry, devastated. But nowhere near as bad as her. She looked up and grinned. Her eyes! Those waterfalls made me want to greet as well. I held it together. Then she asked me in a croaky voice: 'Would you do a bidding prayer at the mass, Connor, son?' How could I refuse when the bold Biscuit was lying in a box at the other end of the living room?

'Aye, no bother, Mrs McVitie,' I went. 'Be an honour.'

'Mark would've liked that,' she went, then gazed off into the distance again.

Apart from when school dragged us, I don't remember Biscuit ever traipsing along to mass. Although we did contemplate becoming nine-year-old altar boys, mainly so we could batter into the blood and body of Christ: cheap wine and communion wafers. Yum!

But if he'd have *liked* it, then I'd do it. I'd do a belter of a bidding prayer.

In bed that night I heard the soundbites in between people's sobs. Their voices didn't leave until sunlight shone through my curtains.

Aw, look at him. You'd think he was just sleepin'.

That's another angel got their wings.

He'll get to see his daddy now.

Wit a waste! Whole life in front of him.

God knows how they'll cope way this.

Images from our primary school days flashed up,

producing these mad projections inside my head. I saw him, as if he was standing at the foot of my bed, I saw him. Cheeky grin, wonky teeth, face smacked with freckles. I don't believe in angels and stuff like that, for me, Biscuit isn't getting any wings. Sorry to break it to you, but my boy's going deep into the ground and flying nowhere.

Denise put it on Facebook that the family didn't want anyone to wear black at the funeral. Or green. Or blue. *But jeans are OK.* And, *under no circumstances trackies, hoodies or C.P. Company goggle jackets.* Me and the troops wore white shirts. No ties. *Black trainers are fine, but best if they're white,* she'd written. I wore my Nike Air Max 95s. Or, as Trig calls them, one-tens, cos that's what they cost. We all wore our one-tens. Serious currency, trainers are these days.

I'm walking up the aisle and can sense the troops nudging each other; probably trying not to giggle. In any other circumstance they'd be careering over each other to put me off. This one's a game changer for everyone. My legs are vibrating under my trousers. It's seriously not funny. But even though there's a riot raging in my stomach, I'm desperate to do the job for Mrs McVitie and her clan.

When I step up to the lectern, everything seems to slow to half-speed. Hundreds of eyes glaring, waiting for the action to start. The sound of sniffs, heavy breaths and dry coughs attack as if they're all ganging up. Similar, but different, to when we're battling. Especially those Fleeto cunts up in Airdrie, who'll, and mark my words, get theirs soon enough.

Mrs McVitie has to be steadied by Denise and another woman. I'm guessing an auntie. Mrs McVitie's decked top-to-toe in black. Obviously she's been spared in Denise's what-to-wear-at-a-funeral post. I spy my dad. Sitting, arms tightly folded; black Crombie coat snug against his muscles. Pure bouncer pose. Aye, well, you're not at work now, mate. His daggers are ten times worse than Denise's. As if all this was my fault. Like I was the one that plunged Biscuit. Nuts. I wasn't even there. Poor fucker got ambushed sauntering through the park. Alone. You'd need to be some special shite stain to jump someone on their own. I told them everything I saw, which was nothing and fuck all. Same as the troops, who are now bowing their heads, by the way. Being here is sore for us. We've lost our mate. One of our limbs. People don't get that. The venom in their eyes when they look at us. You should see it, man. I'm not stupid, I know they think we're a bunch of hopeless Neds with fuck all going for us. Aye, mibbe, but not me. I'm more than what's etched on their faces. Much more.

I adjust the wee mic and suck in some air.

'In thanking you for the life of Mark, we ask you, Lord, to accept the good things he has done. And that you may lead him, in your mercy, to eternal life.'

When the words exit my mouth, I can just hear Biscuit's reaction: *Wit are you on about, ya fanny?*

Blame the priest. It was him who gave me the bidding prayer.

If it was up to me, I'd have said something like: *Biscuit was one of my best mates; a diamond. He'd have done anything for anyone. Wasn't a bad bone in his body. All he wanted to do was have a laugh and become a joiner or a rapper. It's a tragedy that he won't get to do that now.*

I lean into the mic and increase my volume: 'Lord hear us.'

'Lord graciously hear us,' everyone goes in return. And that response thrusts a power right through me. That's what respect does. I wouldn't mind doing a few more of these bidding prayers. *Mark would've liked that.* Aye, you think?

I want to heave my chest out when stepping away from the lectern; kinda proud of myself. Mrs McVitie tightens her lips as if to say 'Thanks, son.' Denise is still launching daggers. Utter bin-lid. The look on Dad's face hasn't changed, his arms haven't shifted out of their fold either. I see the troops, a wee bit of me wants to run over and hug them, but, instead, I gently run my fingers over the length of Biscuit's jazzed-up coffin lid as I pass. That slams me back down to earth.

Some coffin, a belter, but honestly, tacky as fuck.

Shrine

'Fuckin' nick of all this,' Nails keeps muttering to herself as she wades through the stuff people have left at the scene. 'I mean, who leaves leftover party balloons?' She boots a deflating gold number eight. 'What're people all about?'

'Aye, some amount of guff here, man,' Wee Z goes.

'Check this,' I go. 'Some clown's left Communion candles.'

'And all these.' Nails crouches and straightens out a Celtic top. The hoops. Rubs her palm over the four-leaf clover badge. Some luck, eh. 'Bet some serious spons could be made here. A fortune.'

Wee Z, now holding a long thin Communion candle, stops in his tracks. 'Nails, you actually thinking of raiding Biscuit's shrine?' He points the candle at her. 'You'd punt these old Celtic jerseys?'

Nails stands, grabs hold of her ponytail and whips it behind her neck. Screws up her eyes. 'Did I say I wanted to blag stuff and sell it on?' she snarls, not interested in waiting on an answer. Screwed-up eyes and snarls aren't a good sign;

seen it since we were weans, right before Nails's about to go yeeha on somebody. And, let me tell you, that girl goes full tonto and then some.

'Did I say that?' she goes, punching out the aggression.

'No, but—' Wee Z tries to explain.

'No but nothing.' Nails tramples over a few bunches of dead flowers, some manky Celtic scarves and heads for Wee Z. 'Accuse me of anything like that again and I'll knock your fuckin' pan in. Got it?'

And she would've, no bother; she's almost a head bigger. Wee Z practically shrinks in his own terror. Can't blame him. Nails started doing taekwondo when she was six or something, and it only took her eight years to become a black belt. Says she wants to go to the Olympics one day. I think she'd win gold at a canter. We all rocked up to the Time Capsule to see her last competition and, no joke, she scudded everyone she was up against. Like within minutes. Every time we went to her gaff Biscuit would tie her black belt around his trackie and start throwing shapes. That boy was some laugh when he wanted to be. No one would even dream about calling her a lezzie now. Unless you were after some free dental extractions, that is. Means nothing to me who she's into, I couldn't give a flying fuck. Trig and Wee Z took a bit of time to get their domes around it though. But now, honestly, no cunt cares, it's not even a thing.

'Aye, OK, Nails, keep yer blouse on,' Wee Z goes.

'You two rap it and stop nipping at each other.' They look at me. 'Remember where we are.' I do my best teacher bit and gesture to the shrine.

'Aye,' Nails goes. 'I know.'

'Right,' Wee Z goes and puts the candle back.

We spend the next few minutes sifting and having a proper gander; lifting and replacing things again. Lots of raised eyebrows and shaking heads at all the daft crap that's been left. A bit of me feels guilty for not bringing something. I was half-thinking of printing one of our Insta pictures, but I couldn't find one without someone either holding a bottle of Buckie, making a gang sign or sticking their middle finger up. It wouldn't have hit the right note.

Now, I've seen loads of shrines online and a couple in real life, but I've never seen anything like Biscuit's. The pure and utter shite that people brought, man:

- Plastic daffodils
- Roses
- White flowers we don't know the name of
- Blue ones, same as the white ones, no clue
- 23 Celtic scarves
- 14 assorted Celtic tops
- 1 Scotland top. Why? We supported Celtic *not* Scotland

- A picture of Tupac and Biggie
- 2 empty bottles of Mad Dog. (Aye, cos Biscuit loved nothing more than a tanned bottle of MD)
- 1 empty bottle of Buckie. (Same as the MD)
- 2 half-bottles of Buckie. (One still full; think Wee Z has his eye on it)
- A picture of Denise and Biscuit when they were wee
- A picture of Mrs McVitie with Biscuit on her knee when he was a wean
- 4 Communion candles
- 6 balloons (3 number 1s and 3 number 8s)
- An Eminem CD
- A picture of Biscuit in his full Celtic away strip when he was about 5
- 1 Rangers top (better not be some Airdrie fanny taking liberties)
- 5 teddy bears
- 1 empty packet of Marlboro Gold (Biscuit didn't smoke, not fags anyway)

All chat and banter stop. We concentrate on reading the messages and being in our own thoughts. At least I do anyway. Wee Z's probably struggling. He was in dummy English at school, whenever he went. There's a deathly silence as we plough through the words. I've zoned out of everything else; all I hear is balloons bashing into each other and cars coughing in the distance.

Fly high, ma boy

You'll never walk alone

Out of sight but never out of mind

Thinking and praying for yeez all

Please Lord, bless their broken hearts

RIP wee man

I hear imaginary wails from his family and all of his mates. Us, basically. Even the bams who did this are greetin' their eyes out. And we all know who that was. Everyone does. But around here knowing who's done it isn't essential; you don't grass. Simple as. You just don't. I've even thought about making a secret call to the polis myself; yap about everything I know. But honestly, if it ever got out that I'd grassed, life wouldn't be worth living, and I'm not ready to press that self-destruct button yet. No danger. Even my dad would go off his tits. No, much safer to be a stabber than a grasser in these parts. Just leaves you feeling angry and hopeless. Some world, man.

Reading all those *love ye, miss ye, too soon, another angel, blue-eyed boy* begins to batter at your insides. You feel yourself welling up, your body tensing. Your fists clench until the veins on your hands pop, until they're ready to crack something. Jaws. Cheeks. Eyes. Anything. You don't know what to do with your rage. You want to do something with these fists. You want to scream into the clouds. You want to phone the polis. You want to talk. You want to shake some sense into this community. You want peace. You want to fuckin' crown some cunt. You want to cry or run. You want to lock yourself in your room and not come out for fifty-nine years. You just want away from here.

I turn my back on Nails and Wee Z, hunker down and pretend to read more of the messages. I thrust and twist my knuckles into the grass, which helps me breathe properly again. My eyes refocus.

I wonder what they'll do with all this crap after everything becomes a *something bad happened here* memory, and poor Biscuit gets shrunk to *that wee guy who got murdered in the park, remember?* Council will have to bin it. Mibbe Biscuit's mum will keep some of it. I don't want a thing. Not a sniff.

'Awright, troops.' Trig's voice booms from the distance. He's marching towards us with his arms stretched out wide as if he's Jesus on the cross. More like Jesus in a grey Kenzo trackie and Burberry hat, which is perched on the top of his dome instead of a crown of thorns. He's grinning from ear to ear. Some bounce he's got in his step, you'd think he was off to a stag do. As he gets closer I see that his eyes are like a pair of Swarovskis; don't tell me he's been on the swally already. 'WestEnd Young Team in the area,' he goes in a stupid Manchester accent.

'Awright, ma man,' Wee Z shoots back at him.

Nails fires me a glance. 'What's he all about?'

'Mibbe he's steamin',' I mutter to Nails, not wanting to believe that he's been swallying at this time of the day. But it's Trig we're talking about here, so I wouldn't put it past him.

'He better not have been,' Nails goes. She hates steamers, nothing to do with her fitness or the fact that she's practically training for the Olympics, she just can't stand how it turns people into complete and utter tools. But, in my opinion, it's cos her dad's always rattled every time you see him. The king of the tools.

'Awright, Trig,' I go.

'Awright, Con, ma man,' he goes.

'Magic, innit?' Wee Z points to the football tops. 'Should see the amount of swag here, Trig.'

Among the lads Trig is by far the biggest Celtic fan. Or IRA head. For him, winning and losing is the difference between a night of shitehousery or shindig. Wee Z pretends to be a football fan, but you could scribble on the back of a

14

stamp what he knows about it. He hides it, but he loves cricket. No joke. He told us that his dad was a bit of a player back in the day. And when you go into his house, which is rare cos we never get invited, there's loads of cricket trophies everywhere. Four bedrooms and three bogs, too. Pure posh fuckers. Dad runs a cash 'n' carry somewhere in the Southside of Glasgow. Nobody's seen Wee Z playing cricket, right enough. Bore the nugget right off you, so it would.

Trig gawps at the shrine, nodding his head in agreement. He's in awe. He'd definitely want something similar. No danger.

'Fuckin' magic, man,' Trig goes. 'Tellin' ye, some popularity on the Biscuit boy.'

'Fact,' Wee Z agrees.

'Me and our Sean were down for a swatch yesterday.' Trig then gently toes one of the teddy bears in the face. 'Our Sean says you could probably make some serious wedge off those old Celtic tops.'

I look at Wee Z and give him a *don't even go there* nod. Once again Nails does her eyes thing and straightens up her shoulders. She's about to say something, but I get in there first:

'He'd have liked it,' I go. 'All the stuff and the mentions.'

'Fuckin' right he would've,' Trig goes. 'He'd have been buzzin' aff this.'

'And then some,' Wee Z goes.

'Shows you people cared, you know,' I go. 'Mean, look at some of those mentions.' I turn and start to reread another.

You wur taken too early bro, but yool
always be in our hearts and minds

'Better believe it they care,' Nails goes.

Trig boots another bear in the face, harder this time. It flies in the air and lands on a bunch of blue flowers.

'Aye, but some cunts don't care,' Trig spits out.

'That's not true, Trig,' Wee Z goes. 'Look at all this.' He swings an arm the length of the shrine and back again.

'Am no talking about that, ya rocket,' Trig snarls at him. He then whips out his phone. 'Come here and see this.' He gestures and we all huddle around. 'Look.' He starts scrolling through some Reddit comment pages. 'Check all this out.'

We read:

Biscuit wiz a wee dick
Geez got wit wiz comin to him
Good riddance to the wee shitebag
Live like a ned die like a ned
This wiznae yer wrong time wrong place
stabbin

BOOM! Another headache aff oor streets

'Fuck sake, man,' Nails goes.

'A bit harsh,' Wee Z adds.

I say nothing.

We can't be everyone's mucker. But still. I agree with the others, it's harsh as fuck, especially given that it's still raw. He was eighteen, man. Still a wean. People are vindictive pricks hiding behind a phone.

'And check this wan out,' Trig goes. 'Found this on TikTok.'

As soon as the video kicks in I recognise them right off the bat. Six pricks bouncing around to some DJ Rankin tune. And get this, Biscuit's face pops up all over the screen as if he's dancing along as well. Worst bit is when they start to reenacting what happened that night in the park. No, this is a full-on roast. A total liberty.

'Thing is,' Trig goes, 'they cunts think they're getting away with it.' He sniffs hard. 'Ain't happening as long as I've got anything to do with it.'

'Wankers,' Nails says. 'Nick of them. I'd knock fuck out of every one of them. In a heartbeat.'

'Can't even dance,' Wee Z goes.

'This is a message,' I go.

'No shit this is a message,' Nails adds.

'Aye, well,' Trig goes, turning off TikTok and firing up his Instagram. 'If you think *that* was a message, have a gander at this.'

Three snaps of the same gang are standing beside Biscuit's shrine, grinning their heads off. Buckie bottles held up like trophies. One and two finger salutes. The works. They're all wearing some kinda Rangers gear: scarves, hats, jackets. Then, worst of all, there's a snap of one of them pishin' on a Celtic top. No joke, man. Lowest of the low. Below shite. Must've been yesterday or the day before. Pics were posted this morning. I wipe my nose.

'I feel a severe bout of revenge coming on,' Nails goes.

'What should we do, Trig?' Wee Z asks. You can hear the fear spinning around his tonsils. Wee Z's many things but fighter isn't one of them; you'd worry taking him into battle with you.

'Well, wait till you see this, troops,' Trig goes, 'and then we can have a blether about what we're gonna do about it.'

He swipes onto some video. It's their top boy pacing about. Burberry Covid mask tight around his chops. Black Adidas down jacket zipped up to the neck. Hood up. Rangers hat peeking out. Nothing happens for a bit; fanny just seems to be walking about in circles. A bull waiting for his red rag. A caption comes up: *YOBBOY*.

'Keep watching,' Trig tells us. We're all glued. A techno beat kicks in and this YOBBOY starts riffing.

Yo! Yo! Yo!

Shout out to aw ma troops fae the Winhill Fleeto.

18

Young WF! Young WF!
Yo! Yo! Yo!
Doin' this puts me in deep danger,
but A thought A'd risk it.
See, up here, we're no greetin' fur yer wee boy Biscuit.
Tell me. How much you missin' it?

Yo! Yo! Yo!

Troops up here will make some clamour,
tell the world how
we saw yer boy sprint then stagger.
You lot can mourn his death.
But never forget this: it wiz the Young WF
who took his last breath.

Yo! Yo! Yo!

In the papers they wrote
aboot his wee angel face.
But that big gub wiz his real disgrace.
So ye can thank the Young Winhill Fleeto
for putting him in his place.

Yo! Yo! Yo!

Aye, mibbe it's a shame
cos yer wee soldier
will nivir git older.
Don't dispair
ye can all pop up tae oor place
an hiv a wee cry on ma shoulder.

Yo! Yo! Yo!

If you think you stand a chance
well, come see the YWF
and we'll have a dance.
Or, if ye prefer
we'll come down
and dance there.

We don't say anything. Lots of huffing and blowing
cheeks. Trig starts swearing. Followed by Nails. Wee Z gets
involved. There's anger in the air. We watch it again and
again.

'That's the worst diss I've ever seen,' Nails goes, breathing
like a knackered horse.

'Mibbe we just turn it over to the polis,' Wee Z goes.
'Mean, that's all the evidence they need right there.'

We all glare at him at the same time. Sometimes you
wonder if he leaves home and forgets to bring his brain.

'Shut it, ya spanner,' Trig tells him.

'Yobboy isn't serious,' I go. 'It's just bravado. Him being Billy Big Bawz.'

'Totally,' Wee Z adds.

'And horrendous rap into the bargain,' I go.

'Aye, well, that's true,' Nails goes. 'The guy's half-illiterate.'

'Half what?' Wee Z asks.

'Never mind,' I go.

'Half a fuckin' brain cell is wit the cunt is,' Trig spits. 'We need to do a reply, our own diss.'

'That's it,' Wee Z goes. 'Belter.'

'We can't just sit on our arses,' Trig adds. 'And pretend we haven't seen it.'

'Course they'll know we've seen it,' I go.

'Well, I'm no rapping,' Nails goes. 'No danger.'

'Me neither. I can't,' Wee Z goes.

'It's a doddle,' Trig looks at me. 'Con'll do it.'

The three of them stare at me and nod their heads, as if it's a done deal already.

'What?' I go. Their eyes widen with some kinda excitement. 'Are you lot off your nut? Fuckin' no chance I'm doing a diss rap.'

'But you were in the top set in English, Con,' Trig goes. 'Mrs Burns always said you could have gone to uni.'

Trig, as per, doesn't know his arse from his elbow; bumbling idiot is getting me mixed up with Biscuit. *He* was

21

the one Mrs Burns harped on about going to uni, not me. I wish!

'And yer magic at making up rhymes when yer trying to be Eminem,' Wee Z goes.

You know, your words are quite dazzling at times, Mark. Mrs Burns actually said that, I remember it well. Biscuit looked at her as if she'd just called him a wasteful wanker. Her compliment gave him the biggest red neck.

'Stormzy, too,' Trig adds. 'Fuckin' dynamite, mate.'

'Good point,' Nails goes. 'And you read books.'

'What did Mrs Burns know anyway?' I groan at them.

She was spot on, Biscuit's words were dazzling, whenever we scribbled together, his outshone mine by a mile.

'Do the diss,' Trig goes, calmly. 'Then we'll stamp their heads like a fuckin' Irn-Bru can.'

I kick the grass, stare at my one-tens and shake my head. 'No way, man. Not happening. You'd need to be mental to respond to that. Yobboy's nothing. He's just full of his own fuckin' pish. And as for that YWF mob—'

'We have to respond,' Trig's voice is louder. 'We can't let these Hun nuggets just get away with what they've done, Con. We've got to do something.'

'Why?' I belt back at him. 'Why do we have to do something?'

'You want them laughing at us, Con?' Nails goes. 'You

want them thinking we're shitebag clowns?' I stare at Nails, craving her support.

'And what are you wanting to do, Nails?' I hear the anger in my voice. 'For us all to march right up to there and do battle?'

'Fuck, aye,' Trig goes. 'That's exactly what I want to do, Con.'

'It's not as if we're asking you to get tooled-up or anything. Or for you to take penalties into someone's napper,' Nails goes. 'All we're saying is that you should do a diss reply, that's it.'

'Write a proper banger, Con, man,' Trig adds. 'Something that they'll have no comeback for.'

'Come on, do it for Biscuit, Con,' Wee Z goes.

'Aye, good one Z,' I go, glaring at him. I've a feeling that won't be the last time I hear the *Do it for Biscuit* phrase.

They're all standing, waiting for me to do or say something. Mean, talk about peer pressure. Six eyes burning holes in my body. Worse than Denise. I'm not their leader. Even so, in this moment my mind revs itself up and goes into overdrive: words, phrases and beats begin to form themselves into something semi-concrete. I'm hearing Post Malone's tonsils in my dome; Biscuit was well into him. And suddenly all I'm thinking about is the best diss in the history of diss.

'Right,' I puff, 'I'll see if I can knock something out.'

'Fuckin' top man, Con,' Trig goes.

The three of them salute each other. I can't help thinking that they've planned this.

I jangle dosh in my trackie bottoms and remember what it's for. Trig saunters over and slaps my shoulders. Sore. Nails does a swirling taekwondo kick that misses my face by inches, that's one of her things. Wee Z shifts his feet and hands as if he's back at one of our unders discos. Trancin' the nut off himself.

'I'm gonna post a message,' Trig goes, 'and tell that YWF mob to come down here anytime.'

'Don't do that,' I go.

'Don't worry, bud,' he goes on, 'they're fuckin' getting it, just a matter of time.'

I grip the coins in my pocket and squeeze as hard as I can, pressing so firm that my thigh actually hurts. Wouldn't be surprised if there is a bruise later.

'Right,' I go. 'I better boost.'

'Now?' Nails goes.

'Got to get my dad a batch of chicken for his lunch.'

'Is that all he eats?' Wee Z asks. Normal question cos quite possibly chicken is the only thing Wee Z's ever seen him eat. Well, that and broccoli.

'Only when he's in competition,' I go.

'When's the comp?' Trig asks.

'Dunno,' I go. 'Few weeks or something.'

24

'You going, Con?' Nails asks.

'Aye, watch me.'

'We should all go,' Trig suggests. The others nod. 'It'll be good craic.'

I can just see Trig watching greased-up muscle men pulling shapes in their pants, he'd belt out something vile and get his cunt kicked in. And probably ours too. You'd only take him to a competition if you had a death wish.

'You lot go if you want,' I say. 'I've fuck all interest in it.'

Before bolting I take a final look at Biscuit's shrine. Wish the bulldozers would come and obliterate it today. That and this whole fuckin' town.

When I'm about a hundred yards away, Trig shouts: 'Don't forget the rhymes, Con.' I raise my arm and flick them the viccies.

I don't turn around.

Diss

He's a fuckin' nightmare during competition. All his focus goes on building muscle and not much else. If eyelids could be pumped up he'd be all over that, sauntering around with tiny weights hanging off them. Blinking . . .

up

down

up

down.

I'm deadly serious.

The living room's like a manky gym: dumbbells, kettlebells, barbells all over the joint. So many bells and not a ding-a-ling to be heard; the only sound is Dad snorting, heaving, pushing and pulling . . .

up

down

up

down.

The spangle truly believes it's a sport, like a proper sport. You'd need to be half-daft to think that strutting about all oiled up in skimpy knickers, smeared in fake tan and flexing your muscles is a sport. Aye, well, if you believe that then charge on, champ. Mean, you don't even get a fat cheque for winning, you trudge home with a trophy the size of your leg. Dad's bedroom's rammed with them; the man sleeps in a gold plastic kip. I keep telling him he needs to make more space; start by lobbing out some of Mum's gear – her wardrobe is still stuffed to this day. His room's a pure midden, reeking of pish and protein shakes. Mum would've pinballed the cunt off every wall in the house if she knew how he'd let everything get this dog rough. She used to have candles, cushions on the bed and pictures of pebbles on the wall. Place was a showhome, you could lick the floors and think you'd just been to a sweetie shop. Looking back, I'm convinced that her hobby was hoovering. Totally mastered that thing, so she did. Still miss the blare of that hoover to this day. When I'm miles away or lying awake at night I'm convinced I can hear it whirring in the distance. Aye, in your dreams, Con. She even hoovered the curtains. Mean, who does that? Tidy-up freaks.

And grub, no joke, she could have opened a restaurant with the skills she had. You name it, she could rustle it up. At Nails's it's chips aplenty, Wee Z's it's curry, while Trig's da just gives you a plate of dry boak (liver and onions or some other rancid shite.) But at ours, it was things like tacos, stir frys and fajitas. No contest. To be fair, 'Biscuit's mum's a dab hand as well. Now, with Dad, it's all about chicken. Grilled or baked. Steamed veg and water. Sauceless. Tasteless.

'Is that you?' Dad bellows from the living room.

'No, it's a burglar,' I shout back.

'Don't be a smart arse.' The noise of pulling weights sounds painful. 'I've been waiting here for ages.'

I kick the door closed behind me and poke my head into his makeshift gym. He's sitting on the edge of his TV chair doing bicep curls. The QVC channel's blaring; clocking what pish to buy, no doubt. Classic multitasker.

'I was just out with the troops,' I go. 'Forgot the time.'

'Troops or Neds?' he mutters.

He changes arm and starts lifting at double speed. The big vein in his bicep juts out like a giant worm. Not the most attractive thing I've seen today. Vile.

'I need to eat at the right times,' he goes. I nod in agreement. 'You should know that by now.' It's a twenty kilogram weight. Unsure if it's a warm-up or warm-down he's doing.

'I know that,' I go.

'Not good enough.' He squeezes out through the effort.

'Sorry. We were just down seeing Biscuit's shrine, an' that.'

Dad stops mid-lift, drops the dumbbell; it smacks the floor, leaving a couple of dents in the carpet. He wipes his brow, runs the back of his hand across his nose then sniffs up what remains; points at me with two fingers instead of one, a double-barrel pistol. Pure rap.

'Don't want you anywhere near that place,' he spits. 'You hear me?'

'But we were just—'

'Am I speakin' fuckin' Swahili, Connor?'

'No, but—'

'AM I?' he growls, before slowing it down and realising he's being a top-quality prick. 'Sometimes it would be nice if you just said yes.'

I don't say yes . . . or no. Best to stay silent. He has these days when his bottle of rage overflows. When he's suffering. Same thing happens to me, but I've no weans to take it out on.

He stands up, tucks his vest deep into his gym trousers and comes towards me. The lassie on the QVC channel is trying to punt a plug-in camping heater. Suddenly my body's roasting, as if that heater is being blasted right onto my chops. Oh, no wait, that's Dad's breath.

'See, as long as you're living under my roof, whenever I tell you to do something, you fuckin' do it, capiche?' Dad sometimes likes to chuck in the only Italian word he knows. Thinks it makes him harder. Nails says it's cos he's watched too many episodes of *The Sopranos*. His double-barrel pistol fingers are embedded deep into my chest. Man doesn't know his own strength. Actually, that's not true, he's well aware of how hard he is. It's easy to say *capiche* through gritted teeth, which get bleached before competition. 'And none of yer shite.'

'Capiche. Aye,' I go through my *un*clenched gnashers.

'So when I tell you not to go near that bloody shrine, or whatever you want to call it, you don't go anywhere near it.'

'OK. Fine.'

Fuck's sake!

'Right, I need some scran.' He takes his double barrel off my chest, grabs the Tesco bag and pokes his head inside. 'What's this?'

'Stuff you asked for.'

'I asked for fillets, not thighs.'

'Right, well, that's all they had,' I go.

'Telling me the big Tesco had no fillets?' His face relaxes.

'I went to the wee Tesco Express.'

Dad stares uneasily at me. I hear myself saying *If you don't like it, get it right up ye, ya cunt.* No doubt he's thinking, *What a streak of disappointing misery my son is.*

'Milk. Butter. Bread.' He slaps his palm with a finger on each word. 'That's what Tesco Express is for.'

'Magic, I'll know the next time.'

He stares at the messages; shakes his head, almost sniggers.

'Only an eejit would go there for chicken fillets.'

Probably not a great idea to tell him I only went there cos it was a spit away from Biscuit's shrine.

'Tesco Express's upped its game,' I tell him.

'That right?'

'Aye.'

'Well, you'd better up yours as well.' He shoulders past me and heads for the kitchen to cook up a very bland storm. I bolt to my room. 'And I'm not joking, Connor,' he shouts, 'stay away from Biscuit's thing. It's asking for more trouble.'

Sometimes I think Dad thinks I'm as thick as he is. Of course it's asking for more trouble. So's watching the YWF spouting their pish on Instagram. So's getting wound up about it. So's writing some wean's diss reply. So's strutting about in this scheme with these one-tens on. So's living here. No danger I'll be visiting that shrine again, cross my heart and hope to (never) fuckin' die. Capiche?

'Aye, I got it the first time,' I shout.

'You want any of this chicken?' he belts, there's not much heart in his offer.

'Yer awright. I'll make myself a stir fry later.' It's a skoosh to do a stir fry. Get your pan piping hot; spoonful of oil, chuck in some chopped veg, pork or chicken, a few twists of salt and pepper, squish in the sauce. Mix. Eat. Magic. Mum's special.

She was, you know.

'Well, make sure you clean up after yourself. I'm not doing your dishes.'

I'm already at the top of the stairs so there's no point shouting back *Pot and kettle, ya dick.*

I salmon leap onto my bed and scream into my pillow. It's more of a growl than a scream, to be honest. Not sure why. Biscuit? Dad? Mum? YWF? Everything.

You think back to ages ago when you and the troops went on a wee robbing spree in Glasgow. Nothing from the big shops that are hoachin' with cameras and screws. Once Trig got caught trying to blag a Fila trackie in Urban Outfitters, he was getting frogmarched into a back office when the screw released the grip on his collar and the bold Trig bolted like a bluebottle. For your spree you stuck to the easy places like Tiger and TK Maxx. Biscuit moaned all day about wanting to get a Stone Island jumper from John Lewis. *Aye, no bother Biscuit, that'll be a doddle, awright.* In Tiger, he got a pair of sunglasses and a miniature shopping trolley. Trig went bananas and got furry handcuffs for his brother, a bluetooth speaker, headphones and a torch. Wee Z and Nails shat it and got heehaw. You blagged this fake leather notebook and a couple of pens. You could tell the shop assistants knew we were on the rob, but what's some speccy Saturday worker gonna say to you lot? Nails would have knocked them right back into sweet sixteen, no bother. Anyway, what you're trying to say is that you've still got that notebook. And one of the pens.

I slide my hand under the mattress to fish it out. It's

not like a diary, full to the brim with who I'd love to ride and how I secretly hate myself; it's just daft thoughts about nothing in particular, wee nuggets of rap tunes that me and Biscuit used to churn out and the odd pieces of this, that or the other. Still, it's off limits, which is why it lives where it lives. Less hassle that way. I know I could just write it all on a Word doc, but what's unique about that? Anybody can spellcheck the heads off themselves. Too easy, man. There's something about pen on paper that's individual. Paper + Pen + Thoughts = Con O'Neill. Might be worth a fortune one day, like that Maradona jersey he wore when he ripped the pish out the English. Some price that went for.

Before scribbling *YWF Reply* at the top of the page, I listen in case Dad's on the prowl. I hear him chanting in the kitchen. *Doof! Doof!* tunes when he's training and old codger music when he's cooking and eating. The notebook rests on my knees, pen tapping against my teeth. Feel like I'm back in school trying to batter out an essay: no thoughts, no ideas, no interest. Even so, I'm trying to think about the most aggressive, piercing thing to say; something full of *fuck yooz* and *come ahead* threats. *You've done one of us, so we'll do one of yooz* type of thing. First I spew this:

> Shout out tae all the YWF crew,
> Think yer magic fur yer cowards' attack?

> If A were you pricks
> A'd be lookin' over ma shoulder an' watchin'
> > > ma fuckin' back.

It goes on for much longer . . .

When I read it my face gets redder with every line. I've played into the hands of everyone's expectations: the dim-witted Ned who loves nothing more than a scrap in the street and a bottle in the park. The thick wanker who'll either die young or wind up in jail. Street vermin. All I've written is an embarrassing spurt of meaningless guff; would be humiliating to have my name connected to those words. Wee Z could do better. Then again. Imagine Dad charging in, ripping the notebook out of my hands and having a gander? Not sure if he'd tear shreds off me, pish himself laughing or just shake his head in the way he does, say fuck all and leave. Doubtful what would hurt most. Disappointed eyes are worse than sad ones. Aye, they rip the soles right off your feet, so they do.

I consider tearing the page out and shoving the notebook back under the mattress, but, at the same time, I don't want the troops to think I've shat it. On the ladder of what's acceptable round here, a shitebag is only one rung above a grass. You could be faced with chains, blades and bricks, but the first rule of being in a young team is that you never bolt from your comrades. No matter what army you're facing, you always charge in. But there's charging in en masse, and then there's what happened to Biscuit;

that was a pure liberty and nothing else. The only exception to the shitebag rule is when you're flying solo, then it's perfectly acceptable to do a runner. Shame Biscuit was slower than Nails's dad shuffling home from the boozer.

Then that phrase *Do it for Biscuit, Con* creeps up again. It's gonna haunt me. Aye, cheers Wee Z for that boot in the blackmail bawz. I try another tactic. Pen at the ready.

> ~~Shout out tae all the YWF crew,~~
> ~~Think yer magic fur yer cowards' attack?~~
> ~~If A were you pricks~~
> ~~A'd be lookin' over ma shoulder an' watchin' ma~~
> ~~fuckin' back.~~

Dear Dean,
Or is it Deeno or Yobboy that you prefer?
Your mum and dad don't call you that, I'd swear.
I bet they don't know what you've done?
If they did, you think they would be proud of their
cherished son?

I doubt they know who you really are.
Do YOU even know who you really are?
Would the real Dean Lawlor please stand up?
Please stand up!
Please stand up!

Dear Dean,

Want to know what I think's up?

That the real Deeno Lawlor is nothing but a

wee scared pup.

But listen, there's no disgrace in that, there's

absolutely no shame.

Cos, basically, I'm pretty much the same

and

I'd wager that my boys and your crew are

part of that mind frame.

Dear Dean,

Do you still see Biscuit's face when your eyes are shut?

Cos I do.

Does his howls smack you flush in the gut?

Tut! . . . Tut! . . . Tut!

Deeno, is your heart broken?

Cos mine's torn to bits.

Can you still see him dying?

Or were you too much aff yer tits?

Cos, mate, I can't see anything else.

Mibbe we can talk about these things one day.

But first, we'd need to chuck the hate away.

Dear Dean,

You should know that his real name was Mark.

He'd a mum, a sister and life beyond the WestEnd Park.

And just like you and me, he had wants and dreams.

He longed to escape the Buckie, the battles;

These desperate schemes.

Dear Dean,

I don't want to fight, have no more blood spilled.

I want peace, joy and a life fulfilled.

Don't you, Deeno?

All this Taigs-Huns-Celtic-Rangers tripe

I don't want to be that guy any more

I've no interest in that type.

Same goes for yer YWF and our WYT,

In truth, I know that's not who we want to be.

Dear Dean,

Let's bury all this.

What do you say?

Forget about us coming up or you lot coming down,

There's no need for anyone to go to town.

So, Deeno, what's it to be?

You want to keep this Yobboy geez alive,

Or are you ready to set Dean free?

I give it the once-over, do a few tweaks and rap it out in my head; still too embarrassing. I slam the notebook shut and fire it back under the mattress. Not a chance of me showing this to the troops, let alone belting it out in front of them. Think about it, I'm basically asking the wankers who done Biscuit for a truce; urging us and the YWF to start waving white flags and hugging it out. The troops would go mental; Trig would probably try and smack me, Nails would swing a foot at my face, and Wee Z would mumble *No way man* sixteen times under his breath and not know where to look. Tense, man.

You lean your elbows on your knees and try to imagine his thoughts in the minutes before they pounced on him. What was going through his napper? Was he singing to himself? Was his head full of the usual Biscuit nonsense? How far did he run before they caught him? Was it quick and painful? You focus on a manky scuff on the skirting board, knowing that if this fuckin' insanity doesn't stop then the next person could be you, or Trig, or Wee Z or all of you. Yup, tense as fuck, man.

As a destresser, I click onto YouTube and stick Nas's *Illmatic* album on. One of the magic things about YouTube – even though it's full to the brim of weans opening toys and people desperate to be famous – it's got loads of these old albums that you can play from start to finish. Mum loved Nas. She was the one who introduced me and Biscuit to him when we were still in primary school. Same goes for Tupac and Biggie. I know, right, quality parenting skills there,

Mum! Initially we loved all the swearing, dissing and gun slinging, but when the novelty of that wore off and the sniggering faded, it all became about words and beats. Some of Tupac and Nas's lyrics are so good they entertain and educate at the same time. Dad isn't a fan.

I'm lying there, concentrating on Nas's words, the beats that punch them out, and honestly, if you changed a few phrases here and there, along with some place names, the man could be rapping about my world here in this town. My experiences. Some of his lines echo what I'm feeling inside; stuff I'd never tell another living soul about.

Halfway through 'One Love' Dad roars from the bottom of the stairs: 'Turn that crap off or I'll come up there and put my foot through it.' I can tell he's in no mood for a comeback so I hop off the bed and press the pause button on the computer. When I say that Dad isn't a fan, what I actually mean to say is that the man fuckin' loathes rap music. And everything to do with it. The clothes. The tats. The teeth. The bling. Mibbe that's why I don't listen through my headphones; mibbe I just want to get a rise out the cunt.

'It's off,' I shout. No response. I'm half-expecting a pounding up the stairs so he can chew my ear off about playing music full pelt, but nothing happens. He'll be in the living room preparing for an evening gym session now that he's inhaled his chicken. Eat. Lift. Sleep. Bit of telly.

Chuck them in whatever order you want, but basically that's his life. I can't remember the last time he was in my room in normal circumstances, without wanting to rip my head off. Long gone are the days when he'd sweep me off my feet and fire me onto the bed. Then do it again and again and again. I can still hear the sound of our giggles. Mum screaming, *That bed's going to come through that bloody ceiling, you know.*

I dive onto Reddit and check out what's being said about Biscuit. Reddit's like a prison without any locks, prisoners running riot and no screws to keep anybody in check. I type in his name – real and nickname. There's streams of comments. Pages and pages of them. No joke, it could make up a book.

Obviously loads are about how he'll be missed and what a laugh he was and how it's broken everyone's heart. But, the weird thing is, I scroll through the good stuff without barely scanning it. All my focus is on the bad. Fascinated by it. Bit like watching people cheering at a football match, I'll hone in on that one angry geezer with veins bursting out his neck. Same way I love a good car crash. That's me, always drawn to bad shit.

Weirdo666
Am glad this happened. Good riddance to the wee fanny is all I can say.

YeahYeahYeah95

If hes 18 and fighting everything that moves then theres absolutely no debate if your into that way of life. Its just inevitable. He knew the consequences and hes now paid the ultimate price. Wee dick.

Heehee71

Live by the blade, die by the blade. My heart's still intact.

KingRib

Another wee twat aff oor streets is what Am thinking.

Special BrewCrew

I've met some real scumbags at that age who managed to turn their life around, but obviously he was destined to remain a scumbag. And look at that family he had, the guy was always going to end up in some box or other.

RightSaidNed

Hes been posting 'mad with it' pics with the troops on Instagram since he was 14 posing with weapons and all sorts. The fact his maw let him roam the streets to all hours of the day says a lot about her.

SquareSausage

I wiz howlin' when I heard. Totally not surprised. Just a matter of time b4 his cronies get theirs as well.

SwallyMerchant

When the news popped up on the phone, accompanied by the comments about him being an angel, great boy and all that, it all sounded like a case of some tragic laddie in the wrong place at the wrong time. Then I saw photos of him on socials and you just knew he was a right wee bam and there was more to the story, looks like it's all coming out now.

SingleMum27

Seems like he's found, in the worst of ways, that actions have consequences.

TotemGirl

A tragedy to see a young life thrown away. On the other hand, all these wee fuckin' numpties fully decked head-to-toe in top of the range clobber and carrying chibs need to fuck right aff.

Tombhoy1888

At 18 you know whether slashing or stabbing folk is right or wrong, also this will probably get downvoted but the kids are wearing £200 trainers, with the latest iPhone models and £600 Moncler jackets . . . they're hardly starving. It might sound trivial but it's a fact, by blaming the local government for this we are allowing personal responsibility to be forgotten. Where are the parents in all of this, that's what I want to know.

SlamFan

I went to the same school a long time ago and this could easily have been me or any of my mates at the same age. Personally I never used a weapon but I was in certain situations where I had one on me. Not proud of that fact, but that's everyday life for some people when they think they've no other choice. Who knows what could have happened to me or one of my mates – *Sliding Doors* moments, people. Life isn't easy growing up without amenities or opportunities. Try being 18 and knowing that the rest of society don't give a toss about you and have basically left you to rot. So don't be too quick to judge. Don't tar everyone who live in these estates as 'bampots' 'bams' 'Neds' 'idiots' etc. Does it make you feel superior? Does it make you feel better than people who have less than you do? One day you see little monsters in tracksuits, the next they could confuse the life out of you and be in a suit. Get the drift? Get a grip, then.

Follow the link below to see what real people do with their time in these estates.

I read more of SlamFan's Reddit posts and each time something different clicks in me. It's as if SlamFan's spouting things directly from my own head; speaking our truth. For some reason I'm thrilled that they went to the same school as us. Bet they knew Biscuit; wonder if they know me. I forget about the bile of all the other posts and click on the YouTube link that SlamFan has put up.

When it loads everything's dark, not a sinner to be seen. There's a rustle of people blethering away in the background. I wait a few seconds to see if anything's gonna happen. Still the darkness. I'm about to click off cos my attention span is between ten and fifteen seconds with these things; finger's twitching. I'll give it another ten in my head. Seven ... six ... five ... four ... then something happens: a wee light pops on, revealing a lone mic stand in the middle of a tiny stage. I haven't a scooby where it is or what I'm supposed to be watching. Tell you one thing, this SlamFan better not be dragging me down a massive rabbit hole of shite that'll take me donks to climb out of. Although, the lone mic makes me think that SlamFan might be a chanter and this link is taking me to all their tunes. They'll get the first verse, then dingied if it's guff.

Some woman hops on the stage, the hidden audience go nuts. I'm giving her Mum's age. Early thirties at best. But unlike Mum she's decked out in student gear. Bit tinkery. Can't be SlamFan, can it? Comedian, is my first thought. Right, you better be cracking some serious funnies here or you'll be getting slung. *OK, guys we're down to our final three.* More stuff from the audience, whoops and cheers. The woman calms them down with some hand gestures. *Each of our remaining three slammers have to do one more poem.* Slammer? Fuck's that when it's at home? *When the last slammer is done our judges will spend ten minutes deliberating before making a final decision.* The crowd chuck out some comedy boos and hisses. Decision? What decision? I'm lost. I feel my face tensing up in confusion, my eyes screwing with deep concentration. But it's snared me. I'm well into whatever this is, wanting to find out who's being judged and what this thing is all about. Twitchy finger is calmed down. *As soon as they hand me the gold envelope, I'll announce who our West of Scotland Poetry Slam Champion is going to be.* She definitely doesn't sound like Mum though. My face grimaces. Poetry?

I say to myself. Po-et-ry? You're telling me all that cheering is for pishy poetry? God, what's the craic with the world these days? This is the exact opposite of when I was in school, whenever our English teacher even uttered the word poetry, you'd think the entire class were about to get their teeth chiselled out from all the groans floating around. I didn't mind it, a bit meaningless and boring, but sometimes it wasn't too bad either. But given the choice of studying poetry or having a right carry-on, well, it was a no brainer. Saying that, thon 'Mid-Term Break' we did in fifth year was semi-decent. *OK, let's put a giant Glasgow hand together for some class poetry.* The crowd do as they're told. *First up, all the way from the badlands of Barlanark is PaulaTik.* Barlanark? That's not too far from here.

The woman shoots off stage and another bounces onto it. This one's definitely around my age. Hair tied back into a tight ponytail. She's got a black trackie and white trainers on. Both Puma. Quality. She adjusts the mic, drops her head to the floor, looks up again with pure concentration – and definitely anger – on her face. Bit of a belter. She wouldn't even dream of looking at someone like me.

Awright? she goes, attitude pure oozing from her pipes. *The name's PaulaTik.* Wee Z would be able to tell you if she's Indian or Pakistani, it's too hard for me, but in any case she's Scottish cos that's what's coming out her gub. *I do poems about politics and sometimes I do poems about stuff that gets right on my tits.* I snigger. The crowd whoop; maddies, revved up about poems and politics. Joke. My eyes are glued to the screen. *This poem is a wee bit about both. It's called 'A Mean, A'm No a Racist, But'.* PaulaTik speaks like people around here. Like me. Like the troops. Like she's one of us. She then jerks her hip and stands with one hand on her waist; with the other she pretends to smoke a fag. If you clocked her in the street you'd think she was after a square go. Reminds me of Nails, minus the fag. Gallus Glasgow in a Puma trackie. My heart begins to speed, I'm a wee bit nervous for her. There's a short pause before she goes for it.

> A mean, A'm no a racist,
>
> but . . .
>
> Hiv ye seen them way their buggies
>
> on buses
>
> dodging fare
>
> clammin' up when applicable
>
> urgin' thur children tae beseech.
>
> No interest in integration
>
> or
>
> assimilation?
>
>
> Hiv ye seen them?
>
>
> A mean, A'm no a racist, but . . .

Hiv ye seen them get everythin' that's goin'?
Benefits for this, that or the other:
unemployed,
refugee,
asylum-seeking single fuckin' mother?
Blaggin' our Social Welfare,
school systems and free health care?

Hiv ye seen them?

Look, come on, A'm no a racist, but . . .
Hiv ye seen them get all oor houses
for thur hordes of brothers, sisters
and spouses?
Babies born on oor NHS debt,
automatic citizenship
for thur tinted tainted set.

Hiv ye seen them?

Honest tae fuck, A'm no a racist, but . . .
Hiv ye seen those cadgers, wey kids on thur back?
They're kiddin' nae wan on:
thurs plenty in thur sack.
Is it a wonder they're always under attack?

A mean,
they could've some English
coming out their gobs
before they dilute oor culture
and blag oor jobs.

Hiv ye seen them?

A wouldn't say this aloud, but
if they can't make it here
wey the culturally convivial
the great receiver
flag in hand
inebriated welcomes
a quid or two
then A fear.

But, it ain't me . . . naw, it's no me . . .

A'm no to blame
for all this vacuous, bigoted shame.
It's they, them and those
you should be tryin' to expose

Ach . . . fuck it!

At the end of the day it's just a bit of craic,
no everyone wants to send them back
to . . .

Where is it again?

Which makes me ex-sta-tic
cos A stand here, Ms PaulaTik,
a migrant, an exile.
Just the very same
minus the nationality
weans on back or linguistic disability.
However,
A'm nobody's menace
A'm received
A speak the local tongue:
ma choice weapon for the long run.

Aye, A know, you keep tellin' me, you're no a racist, but,
Hiv ye seen me?

My jaw is loose. Mouth's wide open. What have I just
watched? Half me's thinking: the pure nick of that, while the
other half's going: I need to see that again, and again. So
that's what I do; slide it right back to the beginning and have
a few more swatches at it. I concentrate on how she delivers

her poem. How the crowd are eating out her hand. How she slowly hammers out *tinted tainted set* while sliding up the sleeve of her trackie and pointing to her brown skin.

I view again and focus on the words; think deeper about what PaulaTik is all about. I think I get it. I've heard Trig's da saying similar plenty of times: *Foreigners moving to the UK to get free hospital treatment and stealing bastarding jobs off the Scots.* His words, not mine. Way I see it, people are people. Two eyes, teeth, a beating heart and a tongue. You can't stop people living normally just cos they're from a different country, can you? Bad craic, man. Thing is, if you're a nugget, you're a nugget whatever language you speak, whatever shade skin you've got. Fact is, there's dickheads everywhere, Sweden, Brazil, Iceland, Sudan. World's full of them. Name any country and you'll soon find your fair share of spangles. Scotland's teeming with them. It's one thing to slag Wee Z about being a numpty, but if anyone goes on about him being a Paki, then that racist prick is getting a bleachin? That's the rules, simple as. Mean, we're always being told how the Internet connects the planet and that, how we now live in this big giant global village, which I'm totally on board with. But don't start throwing verbal shapes and giving it the racist patter when that village becomes a real thing and moves down the road from your gaff. That's not on.

Mum used to talk all the time about us all going to live

in Australia; imagine if she'd realised that dream, would that have meant we'd have been pilfering jobs off Aussie folk? *People are people*, that's what I wanted to say in my diss to Deeno Lawlor. Who cares where you're from, what football team you support, the way you speak or who your preferred God is? Does my nut in. It's crystal that PaulaTik doesn't give two fucks about this either.

I haven't seen the other two finalists, but I hope that PaulaTik cleans up. I drag the cursor back to the beginning again. One last hit.

> A mean, A'm no a racist,
> but …
> Hiv ye seen them way their buggies …

A puff of air smacks the back of my neck. It's not the creaking floor that's the giveaway, it's the boggin' smell. I turn.

'What's this shite?'

Dad's standing behind me with his eyes fixed on the YouTube video. Arms in his usual fold; tense as fuck. Forearms like two massive branches; hairier than a coconut. I think he does this to either intimidate or show off. There's enough sweat on his shoulders to drown a kitten, no joke.

'Dad!' I click the pause button and leave PaulaTik frozen mid spit.

'Asked you a question.' He prods me and it feels like a

drill digging deep into my arm. Man's no notion of his own strength. Well, actually he does.

'Oh, this,' I smile, trying to sound enthusiastic, and innocent. I feel guilty even though I'm doing absolutely nothing wrong. He doesn't look the happiest, no surprises there then. You'd think I'd just been caught red-handed trawling through Pornhub or something.

'Aye, this. What is it?'

'It's just some lassie doing poetry.'

His face looks sore, like he's just been rabbit punched.

'It's a competition,' I go, pleading to the man's love of a competition. Doesn't work, his face fails to change. 'It's called a slam competition, whoever wins becomes the Scottish champion.' His eyes shift from the screen and scan each corner of my room, which, I can assure you, is anything but a kip. 'Want to watch some of it? This lassie's really good,' I go, pointing at the screen. He returns to look, says nothing; tongues his teeth. Smacks them loudly actually, then drags his hand across his mouth. Sniffs.

'I'm off out,' he goes.

Before he gets out of my room I hear him mutter, 'Watchin' fuckin' poetry,' under his breath. I think he's actually raging that I'm not locked in my room pulling the head off it. That'd make the cunt proud.

'And get that room of yours tidied up,' he shouts from the stairs. 'It's a shithole. Capiche?'

'Aye, capiche,' I go and ram my middle finger up to the door.

He's still patrolling outside. I can hear tiny creaks at the top of the landing. When I was about twelve or thirteen – before it all happened – he'd regularly come in and show me old Celtic games on YouTube. I loved going down the rabbit hole with him. *I was at that game, eighty-eight, centenary year,* he'd say. *Oh, wait till you see this, we embarrassed them that day.* Celtic games in the eighties and nineties; being there when we rammed six past Rangers … mean, I thought he was Superman. And now here we are, a silent standoff either side of the door. Should I say something? A wee knock arrives.

'Aye?' I go.

He swings his head round the door.

'Right, I'm off,' he goes.

'Aye, catch you later.'

'Right.'

'Right.'

Tears

I wake drenched in sweat and fear. Heart pounding my chest as if it's trying to escape. Always happens around the same time; when I look up, she's there at the foot of my bed watching over me. I thought Biscuit would've popped up at least once, but, no, not a whiff. Rude fucker.

She's sitting on her knees. Grinning her chops off, red lipstick and gleaming teeth. That black stuff makes her eyes look smokey. Maxwell House eyes. I sit up and gasp for air; always a struggle to suck enough in, but it's what I need to do in order to calm the jets. In through the nose for six seconds, hold for four then out for seven. Got it from that mad yoke Wim Hof. Mostly it works and I manage to get back. Tonight's harder. I'll be staring at the ceiling and listening to Dad snoring the roof off until the fuckin' birds start chirping. Our walls are that thin, you could grog through them.

The chat tonight is her telling me that I'm God's gift. Well, who am I to argue?

Hiya, Connor.

Hiya.

You're so handsome.

Thanks.

I'm sorry, son.

Why?

Because I let you down.

Other times it can be sad. A puzzle. Scary, even.

Hiya, Connor.

Hiya.

Come with me.

Where?

Just come with me.

I never attempt to get out of bed and take her outstretched hand. Probably cos I don't want to go where she wants to take me. More likely cos I'm terrified. Anyway, it's all in my napper; just one side of my brain fuckin' with the other. Life, really.

When my heart stops trying to panic the life out of me, I plonk myself back down on the pillow, do some Wim Hof and feel like a fuckin' eejit for talking to my dead mum and needing to *breathe* myself back to the land of nod. What I wouldn't give to sleep like a wean for at least one night without anyone's noggin popping up.

I'm listening to my breath, counting the seconds. Over and over again. A tried and tested technique that's not working. Head's full of too much fizz: Mum, Dad, Biscuit, revenge and now poems. Wim Hof's some mad spanner. I've a desire to get up and search for more of this PaulaTik stuff online. Or just poetry comps in general. Mean, where do you even go to get involved in something like that? The extracurricular around here is watching Sky Sports, drinking or getting stoned, usually at the same time. I don't remember seeing too many flyers promoting poetry nights or workshops. OK, so they'd have been chucked in a bin, but that's not the point, is it? It's all about opportunity, which we've fuck all of. And when you give people a whole whack of fuck all, it's no surprise when they amount to fuck all as well, is it? Even the one thing that offered people an escape route from this burst-couch of a town got shut down. One week the library's heaving with activity and the next it's a jakey booze den. The brain who made that decision needs a long stretch for crimes against the community. If it was up to me I'd give the wanker ten for cultural and social terrorism. Aye, I know all about their wee tactics of keeping people like us in our place; I wasn't a total fuckin' dunce at school, just couldn't be arsed; that's the God's honest. School was shite. Teachers were either knackered or scunnered; most didn't have a scooby about our lives. *They* couldn't be arsed either, only in it for the holidays.

When I was a wee, Mum used to take me to that library, remember it well. I'd bounce around the weans and comics section while she did her thing. Always within eyeshot of

PaulaTik's videos are still running. All fine. I twist my head to the empty space for a better listen. There! There it is again. Coming from Dad's room. Fuck me, that's real crying, like proper stuff, and it's actually seeping from his room.

I open my bedroom door, hold my breath and pray that the hinges are behaving themselves. Result. Outside Dad's door the floor creaks, which forces my face to contort and my bones to jangle. Outside his door is fuckin' no man's land. This'll be a barrel of laughs if he pokes his head out, how do you explain that one?

Awright, Dad.

You spying on me, ya wee prick?

I was sleepwalking.

Sleepwalking, my arse. Git back to bed. We'll talk about this in the morning.

Night, then.

Don't want to hear it.

I fingertip his door to see if there's any give. At best, it opens about a centimetre. I spy him, huddled at the side of his bed, hunched in the corner. Head in hands. Hands in head. Barechested; looking anything other than a champion bodybuilder. His body's rocking, nose's sniffing. I gawp at him for ages.

You know you should boost, but you can't. It's like someone's hammered six-inch nails into your feet, you're rooted. His shoulders bob up and down, as do his pecs. In fact, every part of him is vibrating. Even his Adam's apple's dancing around his neck. To the amateur it would look like he's taking a fit, but you know it's just the sadness that's inside him. You know the drill. Fuckin' right, you do: the demons will have been hovering around him all day, and just before he goes to bed, that's when they'll come for him; he'll think he can simply sleep them into oblivion, and he tries, with every ounce of his willpower he tries, but they won't fuck off, they never fuck off. His sleep'll be horrendous, dozing on and off for a few hours until he wakes with sweat pishin' out every pore, chest rattling and the demons swirling around his room. And for some mad reason he'll *need* to get out of bed, hunker in the corner of his room and greet his lamps out. All this, in his pants. Oh, you know the drill all right. Your own demons are basically every sinner you know.

When he starts slapping his head, mumbling something over and over again and whimpering like a trapped badger, I contemplate going in. Sounds like the ravings of a man at the end of his rope. Should I go to him? I give it some serious thought, but, thing is, you don't go to a theatre show and decide to hop on stage cos you feel heart sorry for the characters, do you? No, you sit, you watch, you enjoy. But I can't enjoy, can I? Seeing this is a kind of torture; just rips more shreds off my heart.

Please, Dad, don't. Hey, why don't we go watch old Celtic games, ones you were at?

He swigs from the bottle beside his toe, greedily guzzling down the clear water. Aye, as if that'll wash those demons away. His eyes are like a couple of swollen cherries, he dabs at them then drags his bulk back into the bed. This should be my moment to enter, ask if everything's OK, mibbe share a hug before getting him comfortable. At least talk it out for fuck sake. But, as I say, rooted. He fires the covers over his head.

That's it folks, show's over, nothing to see here. Careful on the way out. Do come again.

I'm struggling to sleep. Usual shite. I can't get the image of him sitting in that corner out of my head. It plays again and again. I even picture myself going into his room:

His hand reaches for me.

Come here, Connor.

I see myself folding to my knees in front of him. My hand reaching up and stroking his hair, he doesn't flinch.

Don't cry, I go.

I'm so sorry, son.

Without warning he lashes out and cups my face; his hands are as clammy as.

I really am, he goes.

Please don't cry, Dad.

I hold my breath and think: *What's he got to be sorry for? He didn't make her do it.*

*

I wake to a rank waft of chicken from downstairs. No wonder he's howling like a wean in the middle of the night if that's his breakfast. Obviously, we're gonna pretend that last night didn't happen so we can get on with growling and steering clear of each other. It's Friday so he'll be on the door tonight. I can get some peace, and without question have a swally with the troops. Friday night, it's your duty. And, to sprinkle some diamond dust onto the proceedings, my giro will be in the bank in about an hour; a bottle of Buckie and two cans, then.

Does the bellend need to play his tunes that loud? Pure blaring through every room in the house. Elvis. Utter flaps. I was gonna read a chapter in my book, too. Might not sound like a posh uni spanner, but I like a good story as much as the next guy. Or lassie. Books aren't top of the troops' blether topics, some things are best kept private. We all hide something, don't we? Saying that, I once gave Biscuit a copy of *Trainspotting*, convinced that he'd fly through the thing. Wee numpty stood there, flicking through the pages as if I'd handed him a shite in a bag; chucked it back and told me that the words were too tight together. Book chat brought directly and exclusively to you by the WestEnd Young Team. WYT Book Club, ya bass!

I know all the Elvis tunes cos I've been forced to listen to them since I can remember. Can't be doing with the geezer's voice, especially when it's being rammed right down competition. I'm now convinced she's not SlamFan after hearing the way she speaks. There's no way this woman went to the same school as me. I wouldn't say she's posh or minted, but definitely not from the schemes either. I can't place her. Mibbe Edinburgh. Never been there, right enough. She reminds me of someone off the telly, but not sure who. Her name pops up on the screen as if she's being interviewed. Vicky Rooney. Not a bad handle. Rooney? Hundred per cent Celtic fan. That'll do. She starts rabbiting on about some Scottish Youth Poetry Group and saying that *the SYPG is for everyone and anyone*. Lots of guff about poems and confidence and self-esteem *but I'm particularly interested in attracting young people from disadvantaged areas*. Oh, well if it's a disadvantaged area you're after, Vicky, then you've come to the correct locale. Right, Vic, does having a town chocka with charity and We Buy Gold shops constitute *disadvantaged* to you? OK, Vickster, does having a town piled to the gunnels with deserted junky pads and crumbling high-rises represent *disadvantaged* to you? Hey, Vicko, does a town who plies its weans with pish food cos that's all they can afford signal *disadvantaged* to you? See, if all these boxes can be ticked then I'm exactly the guy you're after, Vickalino. I'm yer man.

SYPG. Got to chuckle. Bet *they're* not causing havoc in the streets, scrapping over territory and football teams. Tagging every wall and garage door they can find. Looking over their shoulder every time they step outside the door.

Sweating in the cracks of their arse whenever they venture to another part of town. Bet they don't give two fucks about who went to what school or what someone's second name is. No, this SYPG mob battles with pens, but us numpties, well, we battle with bricks and have a fucked-up set of rules of how the world works.

Vicky goes on about how *poetry's for everyone irrespective of circumstances* (aye, no bother) and that *young people from these areas shouldn't be silenced or unrepresented* (too right). *I believe it's time for people from working class backgrounds to stand against social and cultural injustice and reclaim their voice. No longer should these communities continue to be butchered and marginalised.* I'm beginning to like the cut of this Vicky Rooney's jib. She's sucked me right into her way of thinking. There's an email address on view, mibbe I'll rattle something off to them. A wee introductory howdy message. One question, though, can you still call a place 'working class' if only a tiny per cent are actually working? Don't get me wrong, there's loads who'd give their right leg to work (me, Nails, Wee Z, for example), but there's a glut of lazy arseholes around here who wouldn't be seen dead in a worker's jacket (Trig, his brother, his old man). Can you? Asking for a friend. Might be best not to fire that into an email.

Vicky Rooney then introduces two success stories of the SYPG. One is PaulaTik, obviously, and the other is some ginger-domed Glasgow tramp in a royal blue Boss polo shirt

(Rangers fan obviously), shell-suit bottoms and manky gutties, which I think were white about five years ago. What's the craic with Glasgow Neds looking as if they've never had a scrub in a month? Pure rampin', so they are. They'd machete their grannies right enough. Vicky introduces him as Gordon Archibald. (Dead cert Hun name. My instincts are never wrong; Hunnery is screaming right out the wee ginger ride.) His name comes up on the screen as Archie. Inventive. Guy looks like he'd waffle down beans on toast with his hands.

First up is PaulaTik, who does something about the Tories being *hateful fuckers*, cutting about *masquerading as Britain's carers*, her words not mine. Still, hard to argue against. Vicky grins like a pure Cheshire when she's finished, *Isn't she just brilliant?* Aye, is the answer. *Right*, Vicky goes, *now Archie's going to let us hear something he wrote in the group a few weeks ago.* Ginger saunters into view again tugging the collar of his Boss polo shirt. Top of the range fake, no danger about it. I'm thinking: what pish is this wee tube gonna spaff? Every ounce of me wants him to make a complete bawz up of whatever he's gonna do. And then he lets rip:

> The Scots:
> Legal contortionist
> Linguistic gymnast
> The Loyal jingoist
> The State's iconoclast.

The Scots:
Plantation masters
K K Klan creators
Slave traders
Reformation Catholic slaters.

The Scots:
Tighter than a virgin's daughter
Tighter than Christ's crown
Tighter than two coats ay paint
The cultural clown.

The Scots:
Us, Them, We, Me
Me
The Scot
In the supermarket
waiting fur ma change
(which ain't so strange).
Nut *change* per say,
or even coins
shrapnel
or brass
but the one pence A linger fur,

                    like a tight-fisted arse

Indignant looks

Internal jibes
Pigeonholed
aw
fae the queue behind.

Pint ay semi-skimmed
Toilet Roll (Two Pack)
an'
Bleach fur said toilet
Left me one pee in the black.

An' a face in the red
as the checkout wumin fiddles in the
                              drawer of one pee segments
Ma shiny little torments.
There wiz no option tae bolt
A lose-lose situation
Leave: yer an arrogant twat
Stay: yer a stingy prick an all that.

In ma mental inertia
A simply hid tae stay; A just couldn't go
Cos
that one pee wiz much better
in ma sky rocket
than in the coffers ay Tesco.

The Scots:

Joke traders

Social crusaders

The disenfranchised emancipators

The great inventors

The waiters ay one pencers.

No, nothing to see here . . . no bawz ups to report. I take it all back, he's not a bowfin ginger Hun. This Archie is an absolute superstar, and funny with it. Guy's full of fire. OK, fine, so I didn't have a scooby what every word meant, who does? Someone's got to keep those dictionary nerds in a job. Still, I got the sense of it. This laddie clearly knows his onions. Not saying Wee Archie *is* Nas, but the geezer reminded me of what Nas does: you think he's taking you down one street and the next thing you know you're in a totally different part of town. Heading to fuck knows where . . . then he brings you right back to the starting point again. Stuff of genius; definitely not saying Archie's a genius, just that he impressed me, that's all. Loved all his gestures too, right out drill school. Glasgow accent banging all the way through it.

Feel a wee bit jealous, don't know why? Could be anything: him getting to hang around with PaulaTik, two of them having a magic time at this SYPG thing or just two people around my age, similar backgrounds – probably skint too – having a go at something that isn't brawling in the street or getting mangled every other weekend. Two people using their noggins and showing off their talent. Who wouldn't want to do that?

Elvis gets louder, even with my headphones on I can make out every word of 'Rock-A-Hula Baby', a particularly shite number, alongside a tonne of others, that seems to tickle Dad's tastebuds. Better than steamed broccoli though, eh. I'm about to watch another video when I feel a scud on the back of the head. Headphones go flying.

'What the fuck!' I go, trying to retain composure.

'What's this pish yer watchin'?' Trig's standing behind, staring at the screen, not a bit concerned that my head's fuckin' stingin'. I clench a fist and press it into the chair. Two rapid is what he needs sometimes. Just a reminder to his rank. How many times have I thought that?

'How'd you get in?' I go, clicking the computer back to its homepage.

'Yer da sent me up.'

'Aw, right.'

'Size of the cunt.' Trig's always been impressed by my dad's ability to build biceps, or to chuck people head-first out of pubs and nightclubs. That's *his* talent. While Trig's the type that would punch the face off Ginger Archie for being a smart arse and having a brain that's beyond Trig's comprehension. Surprising? No. We're talking about a guy who shows way too much respect to my dad, and people like him, cos he can fight like fuck. But that's Trig, big muscles and big talk floats his boat. His big brother, Sean, is the very same. So's his da, who'd have a square go with his own shadow. They all come from a long line of people who're not to be messed with. It's actually cos of his da that Trig's got his name; the man showed – or taught, although teaching's a stretch – him how to shoot an air rifle when he was a wean. Didn't show him like normal people do by heading down the park and firing some shots into tree trunks. No, Trig's da encouraged his young son to shoot the air rifle at passing cars and the odd pedestrian, all from the top floor of his four-in-a-block. Take it back, normal people don't own air rifles. When the police eventually cottoned on to Trig's shooting sprees, his da played dumb, going as far as to give his youngest a few solid digs while Johnny Law stood by, watched and did sweet fuck all about it. At least this is the yarn told constantly by Sean; believe me, you'd never want to contradict or question that guy. The story goes, moments after the police intervention and getting battered by his da, Liam Gunn died and Trig was born. (Yeah, that surname isn't lost on me either.) In truth, I much prefer Liam, but Trig it is. A badge he wears like a one-man brand. Given half the chance he'd happily move on from an air rifle. No danger.

'When's his competition?' he asks.

'Fuck knows,' I go.

'I'd say he's got some chance whenever it is. No sure

about his choice of tunes though.' He indicates downstairs with an exaggerated head nod. I swivel on my chair and face the computer screen again. I've an urge to watch more slam stuff; mibbe show Trig. I'd love to see his noggin after that. He'd want to hook the screen. It's bonkers but in a way I feel like I'm missing my pals. 'Utter pish, man,' Trig sums it all up as.

'What's utter pish?' The voice booms from the door. Dad's standing in a vest and jogging bottoms, protein shake the size of a teenager's thigh looped through his thumb. It's the first time I've clocked him since the tears in the wee small hours. No red eyes. No sorrow. No softness. Nothing. Guy's nothing but a mad humanoid. He takes a giant slug of the chalky shake, wipes his mouth with a thick wrist. 'Eh, what's utter pish?' he goes, with a tone that demands an answer. The belch that explodes from his mouth makes me want to drown the pig in that protein gunk. Trig laughs as if he's just met his hero.

'Yer boy here isn't a fan of the tunes, Mr O,' Trig goes. Dad stares at him with a blank expression, examining from top to bottom: trainer to Burberry hat. Trig would be booted away from Dad's club door in that get-up any day of the week. He's always decked out in the Kenzo trackie and Burberry hat combo. Telling you, I'm gonna have to drag him up to the casualty to get that gear surgically removed one day. Dad diverts his eyes and slurps another slug. 'Says

Elvis is shite.' Nails, Wee Z or Biscuit would never chuck you under a bus, but Trig, well, he'd chain you to the railway lines.

'Him?' Dad jerks his head at me, 'He wouldn't know a good tune if it come up and smacked him on the arse.'

'I quite like him,' Trig goes. Dad raises an eyebrow. So do I. Who needs an air rifle when you can just stab someone in the back? Some mate. 'Our Sean plays him sometimes.'

And in that one statement Trig loses all credibility. His big brother might be many things, and he is, but Elvis fan isn't one of them; I'd be flabbergasted if the stupid cunt could find the play button.

'Anyway,' Dad sniffs, 'what are you ladies up to today?'

'Chillin',' Trig goes. 'Mibbe take a saunter up the town.'

'It's a saunter up to that Job Centre you want to be doing,' Dad goes. 'See if they've got anything for a couple of lazy bastards.'

'You know, these days you can do it online,' I tell him.

'Aye, we all know what you do online,' he spouts and giggles towards Trig, who, surprise surprise, giggles back.

'Good wan, Mr O.'

Away and leave me the fuck alone, ya horrible pair of wankers.

'I've got a couple of shifts with my uncle Charlie next week,' Trig goes.

'That right?'

'Aye, labouring at his scrappy. Cash in hand. Good wedge. Knackering, though.'

Trig's uncle Charlie 'owns' a scrapyard. It's the place to go for any car part known to man ... and the place to go if you want to get your mitts on some hash, coke, spice, heroin, skunk, Valium. Whatever tickles your fancy really. One of these modern day scrapyards. A scrappy that broadens its horizons and looks beyond, well, scrap. Something tells me that Trig won't be carting too many bumpers around the place. But, fuck it, it's good wedge!

'Aye?' Dad goes, face softening.

'Aye,' Trig goes, delighted that he's impressed a man with muscles.

'Well, say hello to Charlie for me,' Dad goes. They went to school together back in the day, obviously taking different career paths. One lucrative and dishonest, the other earning a pittance but comes with a fair amount of social status. Who doesn't love a doorman?

'Will do, Mr O.'

'Right, I'm off to the gym,' Dad goes. 'Then work.'

'What do you bench press?' Trig asks.

'More than you weigh,' Dad tells him.

I'm thinking, *more than you weigh*? Trig's a scrawny wee shite, guy thinks a proper dinner is a pimped-up Pot Noodle. Even I could bench press him. I hold the thought.

'And see when I get back,' Dad points at me, 'I expect this shithole to lose its shit, or I will. Capiche?'

'Good one.' Again Trig laughs. Who knew that some superheroes are decked out in vests and joggy bottoms?

When he leaves we both scan the room. Trig mimes the word *shithole* over and over, his face like one of those stupid confused dogs. Right enough, compared to his gaff this place is like The Ritz. You could suck your dinner off my floor, but you'd never take your shoes off in his. He clocks the picture of me and Mum above the bed. Day Celtic won the league. I'm eight in it. Sun's splitting the trees. We're holding up the same Celtic scarf. Pair of us gleaming with joy. Funny how you remember wee snippets here and there: Dad being absolutely rubber, Mum pushing away his attempts to kiss her. All joking though. The town was buzzing all night. Full of tricolours and Buckie. Think that might have been my first ever Chinese takeaway. Good times. Mibbe, who knows? I've been meaning to put one of me and Biscuit up as well.

'You OK, bud?' Trig goes, putting his hand on my shoulder.

'Aye, how?'

'Nothing, just asking.' And he removes it as quick as he placed it. That's as much therapy as you'll get from the bold Trig. Prefers action to listening.

'What are you up to anyway?' This is my polite way of

saying *What the fuck are you doing here ... in my room ... snooping over my shoulder ... and practically licking my Dad's arse?*

'Fuck all.'

'Usual day then?' I go.

Usual day consists of us fannying about the streets, mibbe hopping between each other's gaffs, playing Xbox and munching on whatever shite we can get our hands on. Sometimes we get mangled if Trig, always Trig, can get his paws on some grass. Sometimes he can get Vallies, too. Nothing better than watching a good film stoned out your nut. Nails doesn't touch the stuff, doesn't want to kibosh her Olympic chances; that stuff can be discovered in her pish, you know. We don't force it on her, don't want her sporting ban on my conscience as well. I've enough on my plate. We might hit the park as well, especially when the giros get paid in. If there's any hassles in the park someone will usually get weighed in. And if any of those Fleeto twats are on manoeuvres they'll get leathered too. But this makes it as if life's blisteringly exciting. It's not, most days it would bore the tits right off you. You'd be better off watching someone watching paint dry. In fact, I spend too much time living in a world of regret or dreaming my way out of my situation; regret being a wasteful nob at school for one. Regret getting dragged into a life of thuggery, and becoming the Lord Mayor of Nedland. Too many regrets to start listing them.

Sometimes I go as far as imagining myself in a proper job, not some mind-numbing stint behind a desk or lugging scrap all day from one heap to another, but a job with a bit of substance to it; something where my talents will go down a storm. Where I can be a useful and important person. Having (work) mates who don't go about battering folk for the jolly. I chill, close the peepers, drown out the noise and picture myself in a smart suit, mibbe a Paul Smith. Other times I'm cutting about like those students in Glasgow. Doesn't really matter what gear I've on cos I'm dead happy. Gone is the vice in my chest. But each time I snap out of these thoughts, I'm usually slouched in my trackie ready to down a half-bottle or cracking the knuckles before yet another ding-dong occurs. That feeling of someone twisting the vice returns, only this time much tighter.

'But know what I was thinking, Con?' Trig goes, planking himself on my bed, hands behind his head, staring at the ceiling.

'Do I want to know?'

'Aye, you'll want to know—'

'Cos?'

'Cos it's fuckin' important.'

'OK, go.'

Trig sniffs phlegm from his nose, which gathers in his throat. Hard and loud, practically hear him gargling on it. Nowhere to grog it out. The manky bastard sits up and swirls it around his mouth before swallowing it. A clatty shebang I've seen umpteen times, he does it when trying to formulate his thoughts and plans.

'Am thinkin' we should fuckin' take it to those Fleeto wankers.' He puffs out his chest, heaves a few hoarse breaths through the hooter. Fists clamped together; face scrunched as if he's about to wellie some fucker. He can go like that, Trig: calm to crazy in nought to five, which is the reason he's as unpredictable as fuck. Once he gets going you'll never see a looser cannon in your life.

'Take what?' I go.

'Go there—'

'Where? Up to them?'

'Aye.'

'And what?'

'Smash the first cunt we see.'

'You and me?'

'Nails too, and Wee Z if he's not too much of a shitebag. Mibbe some of the young ones will want to come along for the ride too. There's a couple of them ready to step up, you know.'

He's right; it's clear that some of the fourteen to sixteen-year-olds in our area have been born with the mental gene. Handful of them are already doing coke runs to mad places in Scotland, down by the coast and some of the islands. Should see the clobber on them. Used to be us back in the day, but we're too old now. And none of us made nearly as much wedge as these wee nuggets are making.

I lean forward in my chair; do a few Wim Hofs.

'Know what I think, Trig?'

'What?'

'That it'll be a suicide mission.'

'That's why we do it in daylight when there's hardly any of the cunts about.'

'Does that not defeat the purpose then?' Trig jerks his head, looks confused. 'That they'll be nowhere to be seen. What's the point?'

'Point is, Con, some of them will still be cuttin' about.'

'Think about it,' I go, trying to reason with the maddie, make him see sense. 'If they're loads of them it's a good chance that they'll be tooled-up.'

'Aye, and we'll be tooled-up as well.'

I almost fall back on my chair. No, sorry troops, no sense or reason happening here today.

'We won't get out of there alive, Trig. We'll get fuckin' murdered.'

'So, you're just gonna let them get away with what they did to Biscuit?'

I grimace. That's the phrase, among a glut of others, that hits a nerve. Hits everybody's weak spot. Comes and will keep on coming.

'Erm . . . Did I say—?'

'You're OK with doin' nothin' about that, are you?'

'No, but—'

'No, but fuck all, Con. We need to do this for the wee man, know what I mean?'

If I did have a picture of me and Biscuit on the wall, Trig would've nodded towards it.

'Aye. Course I know what you mean.'

'Aye, well, fuckin' right then. We're doin' it.' He's got that aggressiveness in his tone when you sense that all he's hearing is white noise. That's when you know not to argue your case and dispute the shite that he spouts. He's right on the edge.

My heart's rattling, palms pishin' sweat. I can't see it but I know my face is the colour of ash. It's not that I'm shittin' it about going up their patch, just don't want to do it. Don't want any part of it. Not now. Not anytime. Completely done with all this crap. I want to start wearing fuckin' jeans, so I do. Mibbe do my hair in a different style from time to time. But most of all I'm sick to death with people telling me what I should and shouldn't do, how I should and shouldn't act, how I should and shouldn't feel. I know how the fuck I feel. Honest to God, man, done with it all.

Who am I kidding, *I'm not shittin' it*? I'm fuckin' petrified.

'I'm doin' that diss thing, aren't I?' I tell him.

'What, and you think a few words'll make the Fleeto shite themselves?'

'It's a message.'

'Words are just words. They mean nothin', Con. I've thought about it.'

'That right?'

'Aye. Words do fuck all.'

'In your opinion mibbe,' I go.

'Words don't change the world, Con.' He raises up two clenched fists. 'These fuckin' do but.'

I rub my face cos there's nothing else I want to say. It's like talking to a waft of smoke. Wee voice in my head is going: *Tell him to fuck off, Con, son.*

'Even my old man said we need to do something,' Trig adds. I remove my hands from my face, give him some stare and a half. Now for his ace card. 'Or they'll be walkin' all over us forever.'

Forever? What does that even mean? Forever doesn't exist. Everything's about now or the morra. So shove *forever* right up your arse. It's not the time to tell him that I've zero intention of being in this dump *forever*.

'Your da?' I go, venom in the voice. Is this what my life's come to? Taking advice from Trig's da! I get chibbed in the throat and my head kicked in cos Trig's da told us to go up there and *take it to them*? The poor cunt was so worried we might lose face that he sent his son and all his chums up the Fleetoland to sort them out? Is this some sort of piss-take? Mean, the noggin boggles; whose father in their right mind advises their youngest child to go into battle? Well, Trig's, that's whose. And all this expert advice coming from the type of brain power who'd fix an ashtray to a motorbike. Trig's da! I wouldn't ask that cunt for directions if I passed him in the desert. Know what? I wouldn't be surprised if he wanted to tag along for the craic. Tooled-up, naturally.

'Your da?' I say again with a sardonic chuckle this time.

'Aye, that's right, my da.'

'And what the name of fuck has he got to do with it?'

'He knows the score, Con. That's what he has to do with it.'

'What's his big plan then?'

'That we stop fuckin' about, march right up there and kick some heads in. Give a bit back. Get some revenge.'

'Revenge?'

'Aye, revenge.'

I tug at the hair on the back of my neck. Revenge. That's all people are looking for these days. Dad wants it for Mum, even if he doesn't know it. Denise wants it for her brother, against us. Primarily me. Nails wants it against her da, who's one of the biggest rockets you'll ever meet, and Biscuit's mum, I'd say, wants it against her God.

And me? Well, I want it for everything. Revenge, it'll strangle us all in the end.

'And what will revenge lead to, Trig?' He stares at me. Be-fuckin-fuddled. 'It's not a quiz.'

'You tell me.'

'More revenge, that's what it'll lead to.'

'And what of it?'

'So, it'll never end, will it? It'll keep being this tit for tat shite until we've no idea what the original tit for tat shite was.'

Trig stands, fixes his hat and starts twisting one of his rings.

'What the fuck are you on about, Con? We're just gonna crack a few skulls for Biscuit. It's not fuckin' let's analyse the world, is it?'

And there it is again, *for Biscuit.* Tell you something for nothing, my life won't be determined cos that spangle got himself murdered. No fuckin' danger, it's not. I look to the ceiling and say, *Didn't mean that, Biscuit,* in my head.

'So, have you got a plan then? Or is everything based around just goin' up there mob-handed?'

It's obvious he's put as much planning into this as he has about taking a shite; only this shite's coming out of a different hole. I can practically see his brain going into overdrive trying to come up with something that seems well thought out; his napper full of wee motors crashing into each other.

'Aye,' he goes. 'We'll meet start of next week to discuss plans and strategy. Monday or Tuesday, don't want to waste the weekend.'

I almost laugh. Strategy! Fuckin' tube has the middle of a doughnut for a brain. Dipshit thinks he's in the SAS.

'Thought you had a few shifts with yer uncle Charlie next week?'

'Aye, but it's flexible,' he winks. 'Know what I mean?'

Oh, aye, a hundred per cent I know what you mean, Trig. Me old china.

'Have you told any of the others about this great idea?' I ask.

'You're the first.'

How to make a guy feel special, cheers.

'Magic,' I go and swivel back around to face the screen again. Can't be doing with him hovering over me. Think I'd rather see Ginger Archie again . . . bet he'd have a plan up the sleeve of his fake Hugo Boss.

'Stick some Drake on, or somethin',' he goes.

'No chance,' I tell him, just to be on the rotten side. 'I want to hear Kano.' Trig hates Kano. He's into megastars and heavy beats.

When Kano kicks in it drowns out his horse breathing.

'What was that pish you were watchin' when I first came in?'

'Nothin', just footerin' about on YouTube. Took me on a wee trip, you know what it's like.'

'Some amount of shite on that thing.'

'Aye.'

I sense he's restless: pacing, twirling and twisting his rings. It can't be Kano. Something else. I'm guessing Sean. Thank fuck I don't have a big brother who uses me as a punchbag whenever he's steaming. Trig's taken a right few sore ones off Sean ever since I've known him; reasons range from just being in the room to farting. But usually it's cos Trig's said something to make Sean explode.

Run and get me twenty fags, ya wee prick.

Aye, watch me.

Zat right?

SCUD! Two rapid to the side of Trig's head.

Could be his da as well. Definitely not girl stuff, Trig couldn't get a bird in an aviary. Can't be the impending scrap with the Fleeto cos Trig adores a battle.

I clock the time, well after ten. Time to search the Job Centre website. You never know, sometimes miracles do happen.

'Right,' he nudges me on the shoulder. 'What are we doin' the day?'

'I'd better get this place tidied up.'

'Place is spotless.' Trig gestures around the room. 'Come on, we'll cut about and see what the craic is.'

What an offer. Christ almighty. Aye, let's roam the streets, Trig. That sounds like a hoot. I'm well up for that.

'You heard him earlier,' I go. 'He'll lose his shit if I don't.'

'Aye,' he goes, resigned to the fact that he'll have all the craic to himself. 'Right enough, Con, you wouldn't want to be on the other end of a backhander from yer da.' Trig flicks his eyes to the screen. 'Any brain surgeon jobs goin'?'

'Fuck all. Usual.'

Eight thousand numpties applying for a single cleaning job. What's the point? Bet the middle class aren't applying for these jobs; no, it's only us clowns who do that cos we're just here to serve the rich. Mean, who the fuck else is gonna scrub shite off their bogs, wash their windows or deliver their Amazon pish? It's people from around here who do that on a daily basis then bus it back to their tiny gaffs, shattered, raging and miserable. A life of struggle. Saw it all the time with Mum. Call that living? It's like existing in a massive open prison with zero possibility of escape. And know the worst thing about it is? All they posh twats are laughing at us. Aye, those who've never set foot in an area like ours, are pishin' themselves from a high height at the poor wee dregs who should've stuck in at school. They think it's *us* who need *them*, but the reality is, it's those fuckers who need us, cos without us they'd be well and truly fucked. Any wonder how the uncle Charlies of this world are created?

'Right, I'll catch you later then, Con.'

'No bother.'

'Giros'll be in soon anyway.'

'True.'

'Let's get mad way it the night.'

'Send me a text later.'

I'm relieved when the door slams shut. When you live in a place where the popular phrase for saying 'let's have a drink' is likened to madness, you know that the cards you've been dealt in life have booted you firmly in the bawz. Who the fuck in their right mind wants to get *mad way it*? You'd need to be nuts to even want to be mad. Violence. Aggression. Saving face. Scunnered with it all. Too much pressure.

Since the wee man died, you feel that you haven't had a chance to catch a breath and miss him; like properly miss him. Whatever that means. Mostly when you think about it, what you feel is guilt and not much else. Riddled top to toe with it. For the first few days you're convinced that the door'll go and he'll be standing there, a wad of freckles and swagger. Every time your phone pings there's that split-second when you expect he's sent you through a right belly laugh. But then it scuds you again and you quickly realise that stuff like that will never happen again; in fact, it's taken a while to realise that *never* does mean never, and then you have to try and process that all over again.

He's never coming back.

You'll never see him again, or each other's weans.

You'll never get to do any of the things you dreamed up together.

Never be that Best Man you always spoke about.

Dead similar to Mum: never, never, never.

Thing is, you've still got all this love for him, it's dead deep and swimming around inside you, but it's got nowhere to go. Mean, what the fuck do you do with that? Who do you tell? Aw, and this guilt! This guilt'll kill you if you continue to let it haunt you all the time. We all know how badly you wanted to hold him and wipe the terror from his eyes. And how being with him in those last moments would've somehow made things less scary for him. It's not true. At least he wouldn't have been alone, you tell yourself.

Your job now, son, is to cobble together a plan of action and drag yourself out of this quicksand. Don't allow this town to drown you in its giant tank of treacle like it's done with countless others.

I sit at my computer and stare at the SYPG homepage for ages and ages, clicking on nothing. Haven't a clue what to do with my thoughts, how to go about organising them. They're piling up on each other, stack after stack. Head like an Amazon warehouse at Christmas. It's not a case of *if* they fall, it's a matter of *when* ... and where will I be when that happens. Even Dad wouldn't be able to lift the weight that's sitting on my chest. This'll need a lot more than brute strength alone.

A sudden urge comes over me. I want to cry. I'm here on my own anyway, so why not. That's exactly what I do. A torrent of tears. They almost flood my room. I want Dad to come in, snake his arms around my body and squeeze the pain out of every pore in my system. That's what I should've done for him when he was greetin' his lamps out, but, like the fuckin' rebel idiot I am, I did heehaw.

Me, The Scot:

The tooled-up low flyer

Mr hopeless bedroom crier.

Belonging

Feel like spewing my ring all over the rail tracks. Head's like a rat's arse. It's nine bells on a Sunday morning, course I'm throbbing; hangover from hell. The troops *got mad way it* Friday and Saturday. Giro's almost decimated. Not a chance am I wasting any more buying a return ticket. No danger. I've got fare-dodging down to a fine art form, been at it since I've been in long trousers.

Should be lolling around in my scratcher at this time in the morning but here I am, sashaying about Sunnyside station in search of the tiniest bit of wind to kiss my coupon and cool me down. Sweat's lashing off of me. Scottish summer, Baltic at midday, Bahamas at five past. You wouldn't know what clobber to stick on from one day to the next.

I stand up at the back of the station, away from the entrance, in case I'm clocked. Hood up, shades on. Covering all weather bases. If any of the troops appear – which they won't cos guaranteed they'll be snoring and farting the heads off themselves – I've got a ready-made excuse. *Goin tae visit my mum's sister. My aunt Catherine. She's in the Merchant City.*

Mention Mum and they back off like a pack of hyenas when the lions come to town. Let's just say they don't have the stomach for it, none of them can dig that deep into the emotion of it all. Mean, it's been four years. I don't mind talking to them about it. They do though.

On the train a can of Monster helps take the edge off. Blood starts flowing again, body temperature settles. Every time I'm rattling as bad as this, I spout the same old shite: *That's me done; totally putting the kibosh on this boozing lark.* And I mean that. I really do. Cos if nothing else it tastes mingin? But I pretend otherwise; it's still guzzle guzzle or taking dummy slugs – if you're being watched – and fake the enjoyment. It's rank. The odd bottle of Bud is doable, but Buckie's like a vile cough mixture. It's as if razor blades are sliding down your gullet. No joke. Everyone swallies it here cos it's as cheap as chips and gets you absolutely blootered. I'll guarantee that no one likes it; go to my grave with that belief. You can easily lose four to six hours of your life on the stuff. I'm living proof. Doesn't stop me from tanning a bottle, or half, every other weekend though, does it? Braindead. Who, me?

Usually, you'd never fly solo on the train into Glasgow cos at any given stop you could be faced with the appearance of a proper mad squad. Bunch of East End nutters from Easterhouse or Garrowhill. There's not a platform at any station where some poor cunt hasn't been plunged. Happens all the time. And me, alone, draped in this gear, I'd be a sitting duck for any young team hopping on. I'm OK now cos it's Sunday morning, a kinda unofficial truce day in the schemes. The troops' day of rest. Although that's not to say I haven't got the old antenna up whenever the train pulls into each stop. Another new scheme increasing the old anxiety levels. Got to have your exit strategy planned well in advance. This isn't my first rodeo, you know.

As the train trundles into High Street, I spy a couple of guys standing on the platform: both decked in Stone Island anoraks, black and red. Rich geezers. When the train deflates to a stop the carriage chucks me forward a bit. My heart picks up pace. I take my feet off the seat across and get myself into attention mode. Zip up my jacket, fasten all pockets and make sure my phone's tucked away inside one of them, safe against my chest. Now I'm comfortably seated in my 'come ahead' position. Two of them, same build as me. If needs be, I could easily launch a few haymakers and Nails kicks until the safety of Queen Street.

When the train's brakes whoosh to a complete halt I keep eyeballing them. In the pause between that full stop and the doors opening my mind visualises the scenario: take the pair of them off-guard; smack red Stone Island on the temple, that should stun the prick. Then volley black Stone Island flush in the bawz. Remember to check their hands; always check their hands. The *beep beep beep* of the door echoes what my insides are up to: alert time. I keep my eyes on those doors. My breathing is sharp and shallow, where the fuck is Wim Hof when you need the cunt?

They step on and turn left. Away from where I'm perched, which doesn't always mean cast-iron safety, amateur hour if you think that way. They could very well be moving into that position in order to formulate their action plan. Been that soldier before. As much as they've taken me by surprise, I've shocked them, too. I'm betting that they didn't expect to clock a foe on the Sunday morning choo-choo. Last thing they're wanting is a scrap on a train. Ditto to that. My phone pings against my heart which sends a tiny vibration right through me. Makes me jump. I don't check it. Don't take my eyes off the back of their heads. It's only when I see a couple of backpacks dangling from their shoulders that I try to relax. Stick my feet back up, wipe my hands on the carpet-covered seat and whisper 'Thank fuck for that.' See, those backpacks are a giveaway. No squad, young team or gang member would be seen dead lugging a fuckin' backpack around with them. Unless it's full of weapons or swally, even at that, unless you're desperate to get locked up, you're never gonna be train-hopping with swag like that on you. When I get a better swatch this pair look too clean-cut for any toe-to-toe action. Far too healthy-looking; definitely get a regular hit of five-a-day rattled into them.

The doors skid to a close. Train slides away from High

Street. While I'm cool, certain that no punches will be thrown, I can't stop panting. Panting like I've just bolted from the polis. My breathing is all over the shop. Can't seem to calm the jets; it's a bad day when you can't even take a train journey without worrying about getting your cunt kicked in. This isn't living, this is existing on the sharp edge ... of everything. At this rate I'll be confined to my bedroom until I'm around Dad's age. Mibbe it's just the remnants from the weekend's session? The DTs? Think that can of Monster I sank has created one; confidence so bad that I'm feeling guilty about dodging the fare, thinking how everything in my life is all about the dodge. The fraud. The con. The scam. If there's any wool to be pulled over someone's pipes, then give Con a buzz and he'll sort you out. What a reputation to have. Shame added to the guilt. Jesus, Mary and Fuck Sake.

But today, well, today could be the first day of my life.

At Queen Street the disabled barrier always stays open for that wee bit longer than the normal ones. You fire right in after some old dear. Skoosh. Nobody bats an eyelid. Most train guards at the stations give zero fucks anyway. Stone Islanders flick their tickets and the barrier swipes open for them. Course it does. Definitely carting laptops in those backpacks. MacBooks, mibbe. Dear stuff. Bet if Trig was here, he'd want to ambush them. He would, cert. Wee Z would know where to punt them. He's got about a million cousins who'd take anything off his hands. He'd promise a decent price then come back with his pockets full of peanuts. You watch Stone Islanders exit the station and head in the direction of George Square.

Glasgow. The Big Smoke. Grim and gorgeous, clean and boggin' in equal measure. Full of flush fuckers and pure tramps. Always think the place smells of fags, kebabs and make-up. In and out of the shops, people look at you as if you're utter scum; you're always given a wide berth. You'd never saunter around any of the clothes shops on your own cos of the belittling looks. What's the point of going into Cruise, Fred Perry or Nike? You can't afford anything. Shops depress the life out of you, make you realise what you lack; seeing people trying on gear that you can only dream of owning. Mibbe if the troops *were* here, it'd be a different matter and you'd have a rare old gander. Still, you're happy not to be on the rob.

Got to Google map it, cos I haven't a clue where the place is. Only know the crumbs of Glasgow. Some no-go areas, bits around Celtic Park and the big shopping parts. I've got forty-odd minutes to spare so I shoot into the big Waterstones up Sauchiehall Street. The times I've ventured into Glasgow alone, which haven't been many, I've always ended up stoating around in here.

No one'll give you the sideways look in Waterstones. You'll be taken for one of those guys on the train. A responsible young man. A respectable young chap. An intelligent and well-mannered young fella. Uni material. *There's some future awaiting you, son.* You're in a bookshop, OK, so you're not exactly a slinky bookworm, but it's clear that you actively read … therefore … you're not a societal threat. Safe as houses. One of us. All browsers can breathe again. Funny how these tiny symbols can say so much about people, isn't it? Mean, cart a Waterstones bag around and someone will sit beside you on the train, no bother at all. But substitute that for a faded Aldi number, then you'll have two seats to yourself any day of the week. Uppity cunts crossing the road to avoid you and stuff. See it every day. Every single day.

I fire up the two flights of stairs to the Poetry section and start scanning the shelves as if I'm in total control and know exactly what I'm searching for. Newsflash: I don't. Don't even know where the bogs are. Like a library, I've always loved the calming pace of a bookshop: a wee oasis from the chaos outside. And dead secure. Place to be if you want to avoid a battle. Phone pings against my chest again. Probably Nails or Trig dying to review the weekend's tricks. I ignore it. This is my day.

Poetry section's bigger than I thought. A glut of poets out there, isn't there? Who'd have thought it? Scottish section among them, too. Never heard of any of these writers in my puff before, not even from school. I finger some of the spines

grew up in Akron, Ohio and went to Princeton University. To be honest I have to read it three times for it to sink in. Not sure how to read it, do I read it like a book or aloud like PaulaTik and Ginger Archie? Never been taught. Well, I have, but I preferred the old daydream. I think I've an idea of what Jaylen Barber is spouting on about. Wouldn't exactly put it up for a slam event though. Ha, listen to me, heard a couple of slammers a few days ago, now I'm swanning about the poetry section at Waterstones, reading a few dinky lines in one book and suddenly I'm a fuckin' slam poetry expert. Stick to the daydream. A teen with a load of opinions, and zero facts. Gallous . . . or wanker?

Gonna be honest with you, I do a quick skim, solid enough one, and notice that the place is practically dead. Just me and some student looking geek at the far end of the floor, getting a hard-on over the stacks of Graphic Novels. A couple of pensioners fannying about the New Titles and a woman pushing a pram, looking as if she's sleeping standing up. For a split I thought she was about to keel over. Place is deserted as fuck. But, more importantly, not a Waterstones' employee in sight. Unmanned till. I give the floor a good going-over again and genuinely contemplate nicking *Slam Them to the Ground.* It would fit perfectly down my trackie bottoms or inside my jacket, under armpit, no bother at all. I skulk away from the Poetry and head towards Scottish Fiction with *Slam Them to the Ground* gripped tightly in my hand. This would be one of the easiest blags ever; don't think there's any security in the shop at this time on a Sunday. Big mistake with someone like me cutting about.

You hurtle down two flights with a spring in your step, confident as you'll ever be. You're about to liberate *Slam Them to the Ground* and give it a new home; squeeze it under your mattress along with the other stuff that's been living under there. The light from the mid-morning sun is shooting through Waterstones' main door, one of which is wide open. You feel fresh air on your face. It's nice. Welcome. That's how close you are; ten more steps to freedom. Each time you've riffled something from a shop, this is the exact stage when the adrenalin kicks in. Exhilaration mixed with dread – exactly like when you'll *march right up* to their patch or every other time you've been battling. You've always loved that sensation: how time appears to stand still and everything's in slow motion, how your body seems as if it's functioning on electric currents only; you want to bolt just as much as you want to beast right into them with your fists flailing. Fight or flight, isn't that what they call it? The in-between period that's to die for.

Come on, you're a fuckin' legend at this, you've got tons of on-the-rob experience, and let's not forget, the older you get, the more expert you'll become. There'll be no item or shop in this city that you won't be able to crack. This wee poetry book? Well, this is a pish case. A doddle. A refresher course.

Do it!

But, before you're about to exit, you stop. Wait. Think. You ask yourself the question: how is lying, cheating, thievery, thuggery, and the rest, gonna loosen the vice in your chest? How will it bring about the change you're after? You could easily get caught. Not a given, but it happens. Fifty-fifty. Consider that for a minute before making your next move. Fine, so you like that breeze on your coupon, but one toenail onto Sauchiehall Street and your tea's out, boy. How the fuck do you think you're gonna unstick yourself from the treacle if all you're gonna do is keep diving into the stuff whenever an opportunity presents itself? Screw the fuckin' nut, will you. Mean, what would your mum say?

What do you think when you see me?

What do you feel when you hear me?

What do you fear when you're near me?

Close to the entrance is a big pile of books. I think of sitting *Slam Them to the Ground* on top. I puff up my chest and blow out. It's only £7.99. Peanuts. Buttons. Fuck all to those who shop in here. But three dinners for some I know. Or three days' worth of living. I could find it on a torrent site when I get home. But books have to be bent, knackered and worn out, don't they. They need to reek of something. No download can touch that. I reach into my jacket as if I'm about to yank out a 9mm Glock, and pull out my phone. As a decoy I snap the front cover of another couple of books.

Then shove the phone and *Slam Them to the Ground* back inside my jacket; both tight under my oxter . . . and boost. Ten minutes to showtime. Don't want to be late.

On the street, when it's clear, I remove the book and the phone from under my sweaty pit. Two messages pop up; forgot about those. When I see who they're from, I stop walking. Both from Biscuit's sister. What in fuck's name does she want? Whatever it is, it's giving me a sinking feeling. Why has Denise got my number?

R u around today?

Ma maw wants to c u.

Sauchiehall Street narrows. If this is a ploy by Denise to try and scare the shit out of me, she's done her job. A poison. Even Biscuit said it when he was here. She always thought she was magic cos she got a job straight out of school. Home Bargains. Hardly one of the top dogs in the Bank of fuckin' Scotland, is it? Although, a top dog in any place she worked. Stacks the shelves, sits her fat arse at the checkout and is loud as fuck on the aisles, according to Nails's mum, who's never out of Home Bargains. See, if you look up *hating your life and everybody else's* in the dictionary, Denise's coupon would pop up. I wish I could find a good thing to say about her, but, no joke, man, it would be easier to find a butterfly in a blizzard.

An unadulterated cowp of a lassie. This could be a ruse to get me in a confined space so she can finally kick ten lumps of shite out of me. Revenge.

What do I write?

What do I write?

What do I write?

What to write?

What to write?

What to write?

Fuck it!

wot time r u thinking?

And walk on to where I'm going. Head full of bubbles.

I get there with a good five minutes in my hipper; wait directly across the road in the doorway to Cineworld. Place is rocking with weans, all excited about some Disney pish, no doubt. Can't remember the last time I was at the pictures; Marvel shite probably. Costs a bomb these days. Someone's having a laugh if they think I'm coughing up that amount to see superheroes flooting about. Sing for it. Mum said we used to have an amazing cinema in our town, queues snaking for miles every Friday and Saturday night. Closed the fucker down, didn't they; turned it into a snooker hall, then closed that fucker down and turned it into an American Pool parlour, then that fucker got closed down and turned into a decrepit empty building where fuck all happens now. No, don't feel sorry for us. No tears please, cos my town's in no need of a cinema ... proper centre ... decent swimming pool ... outdoor sports centre. No, we don't need anything that'll enrich our soul, do we? Just give us a drab retail park, a KFC, a Mickey D's, and tell us to shut our fuckin' traps; get fat, unfit and be thankful.

I'm watching people enter the building with musical instruments. A posh lot, roughly my age or wee bit older. Can't help noticing how differently they walk from me and the troops. No angry swagger or stiff arms. The people streaming inside the Royal Conservatoire of Scotland building are relaxed and confident. For the first time in yonks I wish I was wearing different clobber. Jeans and a T-shirt, mibbe. Denim jacket as well. Even the name is intimidating. *Royal Conservatoire of Scotland.* Royal anything kills the vibe for me. Fuck royal everything, is what I say. When have they ever come to our schemes and seen the lives we live? Know what gets me? All those Rangers fans salivating over those royals; wanking themselves at everything King and Country. Don't these numpties get it? Don't they get that the King AND Country don't give a flying fuck about them? You think any royal is losing sleep cos people in Scottish schemes are living in abject poverty and misery? Think they're tossing and turning every night, worried sick about the thousands having to survive on one meal a day?

And a shite one at that. Eh, you think they are? Are they fuck. The UK's biggest benefits scroungers, that's who they are.

And *Conservatoire*! Never mind what it does or doesn't mean, I can't even pronounce it. I'm only here cos the SYPG starts at half-ten. And the website did say *all comers welcome at all times*. So here I stand. Bold as brass and ready to take the great leap forward. Meet different people, ready to get fitted for my new brain. Can't wait, man.

Who am I trying to kid?

The nerves are sprinting down my leg. I feel more like a Glasgow alky standing here as opposed to a slam poetry candidate. Mean, I'm huddled in the doorway of Cineworld on a Sunday morning, rampin' of drink and totally hanging. That's pure alky material right there. No one walking past is gonna think I'm from Bearsden or Newton Mearns, are they? When you walk in my shoes, you get a sense of people's perceptions and right now, all the weans' mums and dads are body-swerving the entrance I'm standing in, preferring the next one along. Probably the same people who shite themselves if they see an abandoned shopping trolley in the street. Don't worry folks, in another five minutes some big security bruiserweight will tell me to get myself to fuck.

Ping!

Anytime after 12 is
fine. We'll be in all day.

We? I say to myself.

Brilliant news.

Is that Ginger Archie? I'd recognise that hat in a heartbeat. There he goes, entering the Royal building like he owns the gaff. A scheme boy, as well. *On yersel, wee barra!* That could've been me. Minutes later PaulaTik jumps out of nowhere and shoots for the entrance. It's some assurance she has on her; much taller in real life. Mibbe it's her hair that's elevating her, it's not tied back. A mighty mound, swaying on her head, proud as you like. PaulaTik looks like a person who takes no shit from anyone; she has no physical aggression about her, but I wouldn't like to be on the end of one of those bullets she launches from her mouth. Look at her, who wouldn't love to have that strut? Bet she's not carrying sacks of chips on her shoulders; no, she's carrying a backpack, so was wee Ginger Archie, come to think of it. Books. Pens. Notepads. Water. *For the love of fuck*, I think, *what an arsehole you are*. Here's me rocking up to the station with a pair of shades and a can of Monster. Isn't gonna cut it at a slam poetry workshop, nor am I.

Then I clock them. Tip my shades down to get a brighter look and make sure I'm right. It is, it's definitely them. The Stone Islanders, moseying on up to the entrance. *You're having a fuckin' laugh, these two as well?* I substitute their coupons for mine and Biscuit's and imagine us bouncing jokes off one another. In different circumstances it could've been the pair of us, decked head to toe in Stone Island. Who's to say we wouldn't have come here together? Who's to say we wouldn't have discovered this slam shit, just like those two have? Past tense past tense would've could've could've would've. Hard to live in the past tense.

This isn't me. Not my domain and all that jazz. I've decided. Not embarrassed to admit it, but I'm not going in there. No chance I'm giving all those clever cunts the opportunity to stare at the thicko in the room. Not as much as a pen or paper to my name. Can't be doing with their hidden sniggers, their expert eyes. Judging my trainers, the tiniest specs of dirt on my clothes, my pasty-as-fuck skin. You'd need to be a right spanner to stand up there in front of a bunch of strangers and blurt out your deficiencies. Branded, once again. No, not doing it, and nothing will make me.

But don't you see how you're quids in here? This situation is perfect for you, just what you've been searching for. These people don't know who you are or what you're all about. They've no idea about your past or present. Life is only about the present – remember how the school counsellor told you that after Mum? *There is no past or future, Connor. Only the moment you are in at the exact time you're experiencing it.* That's what she said, and it hasn't left your brain. You struggled with counselling, telling yourself it was a lot of shite, but deep down you know it made sense sometimes; really hit the mark on a few occasions. Generally, you sat in those meetings mute, cos you wanted her to hate you, and mibbe she did. Back then you thought the world hated you, and mibbe it did. But sometimes you'd listen. Oh yes, you listened like fuck. Then went home and told yourself the very same thing: counselling never happened cos that's now in the past. And you know the present is all there is. Just like now. So, go in. Enjoy. Forget the noise of home and be in the present. You don't need to speak or participate. Just observe. Absorb. Isn't it great that you can create a new you? A modern, more mature you? The reinvention of Connor O'Neill. These people have no knowledge of the Fleeto, the WYF, Yobboy, Trig, or anything else in your life. They've not seen where you live. They don't know the tales of the assaults and the arrests and the children's court appearances and the hidden books. They've never seen your tears, no one has. They know nothing. Their ignorance is your safety net. It's ideal. You belong in there just as much as anyone else does. Don't let them make you feel inadequate. This is your time to shine and be different. So, go on, get your arse in there and make a difference.

I text Denise back.

OK. C U then

Head down, hands in pockets, I walk towards Queen Street to catch the train. Don't know what I was thinking with this slam stuff, curiosity probably. Seeking any outlet that'll unchain me. From what though? Can you unchain a brain?

Outside Queen Street station I sneakily chuck *Slam Them to the Ground* into a bowfin bin. Fucker thuds to the bottom; the sound echoes.

Tuck the tail firmly between your legs and return to where you belong. Belonging, that's a strange thing. On the walk to the station, you think about what it really means. Does your town belong to you? How are you supposed to know the answer? Give that one to the universe. Thing is, how can you belong to something if you feel so utterly disconnected from it? Where does that leave you? No man's land. And no man's land is where you'll end up soon enough anyway, it's your destiny. Got to start planning our assault on the Fleeto with the troops this week, can't be stuck inside doing poetry homework. School days are over, boy.

Before going left and out of sight of the Royal Conservatoire of Scotland building, I swivel, just to gaze at it one last time, to consider the fact that I nearly made it inside. *Nearly* is a bastard of a word, isn't it? I see Vicky Rooney rushing inside, late and flustered; feel a chill unrelated to the Glasgow weather. Her words rush through me like a freezing wind: *but I'm particularly interested in attracting young people from disadvantaged areas.* I want to punch myself. *The SYPG is for everyone and anyone.* I really do want to punch myself for walking away. But that's exactly what I do. I walk away.

Bedroom

Biscuit's building is this nasty square monstrosity, full of manky maisonettes. A proper grey and rotten disaster of a place. Ukrainians would knock it back. About a million years ago they tried to spruce it up by painting the tiny balconies that hang off each house this bright orange colour. Think Paris or Rome . . . then give yourself a slap in the face. Over time, the colour has faded to a kinda puke shade. In all my years I've never seen a sinner sittin' out on one, they're basically used as a dumping ground for an assortment of pish or, in Biscuit's case, a washing line. If his building had been a dog, they'd have put it down long ago. Bulldozed the wee fucker right between the eyes. Three storeys high; he's on the second.

Haven't been here since the night of the wee man's prayers. Many times I've been about to walk past but didn't, more often than not, I intentionally take another route. The memories are too sore; twisting and spinning around in my head. Biscuit's gaff, especially his bedroom window, triggers these memories something chronic. From playing FIFA on his tiny telly to discovering the joys of rap music to hearing his first attempts at writing lyrics, that room has basically bottled my childhood. You should've heard some of those lyrics, hilarious, but also, quite good. Should've told him that more often than I did, but when you're fourteen, fifteen, or whatever, you've no concept of these things, at that age you tend to only regret the stuff you've done. You certainly don't think your best mate will be six feet under when you're eighteen.

I dodged his place cos I didn't want them to clock me hovering on the street, gazing up at that window. His mum's probably wondering why I haven't been up to see her, especially since I was never out of there when he was alive. Practically lived there. Stuff she did for me when my mum went, too. I know I should've gone up to see her, probably on a daily basis, but there you go. Shame. Guilt. Fear. Take your pick.

My finger presses the number thirty-three buzzer. The whirr of it still sounds like a knackered lawnmower. Must've pressed this same button about a thousand times over the years; it's always been half-buggered. I remember Biscuit's mum saying the very first time I set foot in the house that she was phoning the council to complain. Guess how many calls she's made? Fuckloads. *And the music the council plays when they put you on hold would fair rip your knitting.* Have they fixed it? Nah, can't be arsed.

The chill from Glasgow is still in my bones. But here I

am, cold and jittery. Wish I'd told Denise I was mad busy now.

Just heading into a slam poetry workshop, Denise. But I'll be in touch in a few days, mibbe come up and see your mum next week or so.

Can't get that Royal place out of my head. Kicking myself. Bet they're having the time of their lives.

I press the buzzer a second time, letting my finger linger that wee bit longer. Just to annoy Denise. Fun and games.

No hello on the other side. No surprises there. Just the buzz that allows me to enter the close. A long, dark corridor with hidden nooks and crannies that lead off to bin sheds, storage bunkers and a communal back garden. Nope, never spied a sinner in that garden either. These hidden nooks are junkie magnets, the perfect place for skagheads to get a heat and cook up a storm. A shelter to get right off your nut. Mean, if I was a junkie, this would be my own private oasis. I've hated entering Biscuit's close since I was a wean; it always gave me the heebie-jeebies. It's a right sinister fucker. It's either reeking of skunk, pish or disinfectant. In the pitch black of night, especially if the indoor lights were fucked, Biscuit's close fiddled with your imagination, I could never get the notion out my head that some cunt was gonna stab me with a riddled needle every time I was in it. In fact, the safest I've felt in that close was during his funeral week. When it was rampin' of death then.

When I climb the two flights of stairs, the door is slightly ajar. I can smell something. Square sausage, definitely square sausage. The gaff across from theirs has been boarded up. Mad Eddie, who lived there for donkey's, must have been shipped out. Fanny lost his leg to drugs and stoated about in crutches; sometimes a wheelchair. Pished morning, noon and night. He told everyone that he got injured working on the railway, but we all knew that he'd spanked his leg with so much smack that he got gangrene. Chopped off above the knee. He used to be a bit of a footballer back in the day by all accounts. My dad said he could've made it. But you take that with a giant sack of salt cos this town's teemin' with could've made its.

Apart from the sausage, the close isn't smelling the best. Stale. Usually it was Mrs McVitie who did the lion's share of the floor scrubbing, sweeping up the joints and fag butts. You'd have thought that others would have stepped up by now. Mean, the woman has just buried her laddie, for fuck sake.

'Hello,' I go, pushing the door and stepping into the tight hallway. And there they are. Those memories again – like a baseball bat to the moosh – not of the times I was here playing in his room, but of the night of his prayers when me and the troops had to squeeze past all the mourners. The awkward silences and hushed conversations broken by Mrs McVitie's wailing. Fuckin' heart-wrenching stuff, man.

Tonnes of people we'd never seen in our puff, staring at us with blame seeping out their eyes. The *here come the Neds* looks. Wee Z thought they were all *a shower of racist bastards*, but it wasn't that, was it?

'In here,' Denise shouts in the most unwelcoming tone ever. My shoulders droop, chest expands. Home Bargains not open on a Sunday? She's plonked on a chair, feet tucked under her fat arse. Plate with a roll and square sausage on the arm. Another roll half-eaten in her paw. Still in her pyjamas. Lazy cow. Hippo PJs. You've got to laugh. Actually, you don't, this is what suffering and pain looks like. She barely glances up at me. You could swirl the hatred in the room around your mouth. The chair's in the same position where Biscuit's coffin was that night. The image comes and goes in a blink of an eye. Snapshot of his freckled face; of the peacefulness. I always return to the *It's not fair* thought. Now, standing here, it's *Why him*? And if it's *Why him*, then it must be *Why not me, too*. Does anyone get that there's some serious collateral outside his family as well? Think they care?

'My maw's upstairs,' she goes, without as much as a glance at me. Her eyes fixed on the TV. I look at the giant screen for about eight seconds. Feels like a year. Some shite about American cheerleaders. There's a huge framed picture of Biscuit leaning against the wall. Headshot. I'd say he's in third year at the time, big cheesy grin on his coupon. I don't dwell on it for fear that Denise will smack it over my back. Mibbe that's why I'm here, to hang the thing on the wall.

'How's she doin'?' I go.

'She's up there,' she goes, jerking her napper to the ceiling. 'You can ask her yersel.'

'Right.'

'In Mark's room,' she scowls, before ramming what's left of the roll into her gob. Cheeks inflated and struggling with the sheer amount that's in there. Did I mention that she was a classy chick? Shocked that she doesn't have a boyfriend.

So you head back into the hallway and make your way up the stairs. This is the last place you want to be. You're now missing the poetry workshop you never went to. No point feeling sorry for yourself now, is there? You're here on this gloomy staircase. No need for panic stations cos the stench of sadness is in the air; you knew at some point that you'd have to make this trip. Who cares if the creaking stairs adds to your nervousness, how do you think Mrs McVitie's feeling, eh? This is what selfish pricks like you and the rest of your rabble have to learn. And quick.

There's four doors at the top of the landing. The white paint has turned a shade of piss yellow. Sure, all our doors are that colour. There's a tiny bog. Denise's cave. Mrs McVitie's double and Biscuit's box room. Used to be mad activity on this landing, doors being battered off their hinges. Denise constantly telling us to shut the fuck up. *You, O'Neill, you're the noisiest wee cunt I've ever met in my life.* I stand on the landing, breathing in the air of square sausage and grease. Should I knock? Seems bizarre to knock. Like I'm some posh English twat. I knock and pop my head around the door at the same time.

Mrs McVitie's sitting on the edge of Biscuit's bed. A crumple of clothes near her feet. Obviously they're his. I'm careful not to barge in and gawp at them, or look like it's me who's feeling the brunt of the pain. Standing there like a fuckin' idiot with your little lost boy face on, in desperate need of a hug.

'Come in, Connor, son.' Son! That hits me like a boot in the bawz. I'm still a son, just. It feels wrong for her to call me that word, but it's still warming to hear it out a mother's mouth. Someone the same age as mine would've been.

'Hiya, Mrs McVitie,' I go. 'Denise sent me up.'

She smiles thon strained way, when you don't know if someone's about to burst out crying or not; lost a tonne of weight since the funeral, her face, arms, legs. Even though she's sitting I notice that her tights are a bit saggy behind the knees. A stick of a woman. I'm guessing all the square sausage was for Denise, then; death hasn't fucked with her appetite. Did I say death? I meant murder. Her eyes pierce through me, like she's trying to see inside my body. She then draws them to her own feet. Not gonna lie, it's eerie as.

'She got a tattoo, Denise,' Mrs McVitie goes.

'Nice,' I go. As if I give a flying fuck. In my mind she should get one to cover that coupon of hers.

'Of Mark.'

'I didn't see it.'

'On her foot,' she coughs. 'Says Mark across her toes. Just a wee thing, you know. A constant.' Her voice stutters as if she's only allowed to say four or five words at a time before having to take a break. It's gruff, too. I suspect she's back on twenty a day.

I try not to laugh, or show any emotion at all, at the thought of that toe tattoo. Poker face. Can't wait to tell the troops this one though. *M.A.R.K.* across Denise's mingin' trotters. What a fuckin' homage. Knowing Biscuit, he'd have a red neck the colour of blood if he ever set his peepers on that.

'That's nice,' I go.

'Turkish place next to Asda,' she goes, grinning softly. 'They didn't charge her for it.'

'Aye?'

'Because of . . . well, you know.'

I tighten my lips. Don't really know what to say. Don't know where to sit. Would it be rude or weird to sit down next to her? I remain standing and do a quick scan of the room. I was in here the night before it happened. Helped him stick the giant poster of Biggie Smalls above his bed. Biggie's wearing a gold crown, tilted on his head. He's staring right at me; mad daggers slicing my face. You wouldn't mess with the cunt. No doubt he blames me as well.

'Nice of them to do that for nothing,' I go. 'They didn't need to.'

'Aye, that's what I thought.'

You wonder what you could get for heehaw as well. You should saunter around town telling every cunt who'll listen that your best pal got leathered in the park, and so what price can you put on that agony? What freebies can you get? Batter into JD's and give them the whole spiel, turn on the waterworks if you want a better prize. You might get a hoodie out of it. Name your brand. Christ, you think, why didn't you do that with Mum? Tattoo? Mate, you'd have been able to get a full sleeve. Mibbe a big eagle on your thigh, even. With what happened to Mum, you could've got your hands on anything you'd asked for. New phone. Earbuds. That's how popular the woman was.

'Come here and sit down, Connor.' Mrs McVitie places her hand on the bed. I sit. 'You've spent many an hour in this room, eh?'

'Never out the place,' I go.

'You made some amount of noise, I'll tell you that.' She allows herself a small sniff of a laugh. 'Used to drive me right round the bend.'

'Aye, sorry about that.'

She throws her head up to the ceiling. I was about to

crack a joke at Biscuit's expense but the atmosphere has changed. A flick of a switch.

'I wish you were all still making noise,' she goes. 'This place is far too quiet these days.'

'We had some great times in this room,' I go.

Mrs McVitie looks at me and smiles.

'I know you did, son. I know you did.'

Having a mosey around, it's clear that the room hasn't been altered since he left it. One of the hats he'd up on the wall has fallen. Green New York Yankees one. Lying upside down on the floor as if it knows somehow, as if it's aware how fuckin' useless it is now. A hat without a head is dead. I want to pick it up, stick it on my own. Or mibbe I just want to kick the shit out of it. Next to the remaining hats is a poster of Henrik Larsson, right after scoring an absolute belter against the Huns; he's running towards the fans with his tongue out, Māori-style, arms wide. We used to do the Henrik celebration at primary school, every day for about four years. Competing to see who was the best, or most authentic. I'd the same poster, but ripped it down the day Mum went. There's a framed picture on the wall of the five of us. The troops. Standing there like a council scheme boyband (sorry Nails), all attitude and bawz (sorry Nails). Mrs McVitie clocks me gazing at the picture; she goes to it and runs her hand over the faces.

'I always hated that picture,' she goes, with her back to me.

'I told him not to put it up.' *Who wants to be looking at you ugly cunts every night? Obviously excluding myself.* I did, I said that to him.

'But I'm glad now that he put it up,' she goes. 'It's the only picture of him in the room.'

'I'm glad too.'

'You look like a shower of scallywags in it though.' She twists her head around and gives me a look that only a mother or a teacher could. We look like some tramp rabble, but I think scallywags is kinder. A bunch of Neds about to get swallied and go hunting for a battle would be more accurate. A scallywag might only do a bit of tagging or nicking sweets out of the Tesco Express. If we'd been scallywags, there's no way I'd be sitting here trying to hold back the tears, would I? I'll take scallywag any day of the week.

'Yeah,' I go. 'We were.'

'How old are you all in that?'

'Fifteen, I think.' But, of course, she knows how old her son is, she's just filling the room with something, protecting it against the sadness. 'It was taken up near the old pictures.'

'Aye, I thought I recognised it right enough,' she goes. 'That used to be some place.'

'My mum said the same thing; people queued for miles to get in.'

'You should've seen that place on the weekend.'

'Mum said it was mental.'

She turns to face me and places a hand on the gold crucifix that's looped around her blouse. As if he can help from up there. She looks over her shoulder and glances at the picture again, holding the pose. Could she be talking to Biscuit, telling him that I'm here sitting on his bed, as I've done a thousand times before? Something in me wants to spout: *Tell him his room's a fuckin' pigsty, Mrs McV.*

'I never thanked you for doing that bidding prayer.'

'Erm ... no need ... it was no bother ... happy to have done it.'

'You read it beautifully.' She raises her eyebrow. 'Well, they told me you did, I was a bit out of it that day.'

My guess is Vallies, that's what my aunt Catherine was on after Mum. Dad point-blank refused. Think he was in training, can't be a hundred per cent however cos I was off visiting La La Land myself. I was too young to get something for my nerves. My nerves didn't count; I survived on wits and anger alone.

'That's understandable,' I go.

She lets go of the crucifix and rapidly blesses herself.

'You'll miss him, won't you?'

Jesus fuckin' Christ! I almost shite out my stomach. There's a volcano of tears ready to explode from every cell in my body. A human sprinkler system. What's the answer to that question then? A nod of the head won't cut it. I fire out a giant puff of air, as if I'm conning myself into thinking that I can blow tension away.

'Aye. I do, Mrs McVitie. I miss him every day.'

She planks herself down beside me again and rests her hand on my shoulder. It starts to shake as soon as I feel her bony fingers digging in.

'We all do,' she goes.

I squeeze my eyes with my thumb and middle finger. They don't stop the tears flowing, they don't hold them in. The worst fuckin' plugs in the world. A couple of useless bastards.

'It's OK to let it out, Connor, son.'

Her hand moves to my back and she starts doing small circles with her palm; reminds me of when I was wee. All I can do is howl, sniff and shake.

'I'm sorry,' I manage to get out. 'I'm so sorry.'

'I don't blame you, Connor. I don't. You weren't the one who put that knife in him.'

'Aye, I know, but still.' I wipe my face with the sleeve of my jacket. Snotters and tears. Salty sponges.

'I don't blame his killing on you,' she goes.

Here's me thinking that she'd be streaming tears as well, but she's not, she's calm. Her voice is steady. Don't want to say cold cos that sounds as if I'm a heartless prick, given she's just lost her fuckin' son, but there's no other word for it. Coldness. Her gentle hand-massaging on my back stops. I sense space between us. 'But what I do blame you and the others for is creating an environment where you settle arguments with fists and weapons.' I want to look at her, but I can't. No way. 'The lot of you, going around like a bunch of little gangsters and terrorising this area.' I'm petrified to take my fingers away from my eyes. The shame of seeing her face is too much to take. Cos you know she's right. 'It was only a matter of time before it happened to one of you. Now, I'm going to be honest with you here, Connor: if I'd had a knife in my hand that night when I found out what had happened, I'd have stabbed the whole bloody lot of you. I would've. And if I hadn't had a knife, I'd have used anything else I could've got my hands on. That's what grief and anger does to you, son. It takes away your ability to think straight.'

You sit in the shame pose: head hanging close to your knees. You feel annoyed at her, but you know you've no right to be. You understand why she's saying these things. You realise that it's not anger she's feeling, it's rage and heartache. She's a mother left without answers to a million questions, just the same way you were when your mum went. You get why she's piling this on your shoulders. She's hardly gonna unload on Denise, is she? You're a safe bet. Take it as a compliment, you were his best mate, his mucker. She likes you. This is not an attack; this is her off-loading. Remember, it was you she asked to do that bidding prayer. Not the others. God, can you imagine Trig up there? No, let her be aggressive

that he'd got hurt. We didn't know at that time how bad it was.'

In a fight? It was a full-blown assault, a cowardly ambush. A fight, if organised, has rules. No shanks, for one.

'I didn't know that,' I go.

'But as soon as I opened the front door I knew it was bad. One of the polis was a woman, a wee lassie. That's when you know, cos they use her to soften you up. She's only there for the hugs. Not much older than our Denise.'

You're desperate to say, *No danger there, Mrs McV. Your Denise would never fit into a polis uniform.* You say nothing.

'Aye, when they send a woman, it's usually for something like that,' I go.

'At the hospital, I realised we weren't in the normal waiting area. They'd taken us to a wee side room. That's when I knew it was much more serious than a fight.'

'I've heard they do that,' I go, just to say something. I didn't have a clue about these things.

'A different poliswoman came in and told us Mark had been stabbed, and that his condition was unknown. Then ten minutes later a doctor in scrubs was kneeling down in front of me. Now, I'm no expert in these things, Connor, but when a doctor kneels down in front of you, you know something is wrong. Bad news is coming.'

'My aunt Catherine told me it was similar with my mum,' I go, trying to soothe the situation. To ease her pain, share it about a bit, you know? 'Some poliswoman and a doctor in a wee side room. Dad sat like a zombie throughout apparently.' I don't blame the poor cunt; your brain would be frazzled with that news. If you have a gander at his night-time ritual, you'd say that it's still frazzled.

'It's awful, son.'

I like hearing her say it, but I wish she'd stop.

'I can imagine.'

'Three words, that's all it took. Three words to change everyone's life forever.' I'm desperate to ask. She looks up at the photo of us all again and whispers through her gruffness: 'We tried everything. We tried everything.' I don't twist my head to her, but I know she's crying. Sometimes you can hear tears falling, can't you? She reaches behind, grabs Biscuit's pillow and holds it against her like she's cradling a wean; burrows her head into it. It's the perfect thing for muffling screams. I want to go home; feel hemmed in, a prisoner. A helpless one.

'Want me to go, Mrs McVitie?'

She takes herself off the pillow and returns it. Shakes her head at me.

'The worst thing about that night,' she goes. 'Know what it was?'

Fuckin' hell, there's worse to come? I doubt I can handle worse. What can be worse than losing a child?

'Erm ... no. I can't think ...'

126

She reaches over and grabs my hand, squeezes it tight. Stares straight ahead.

'They wouldn't let me see him.'

'What?'

'My own child. They wouldn't let me see him one last time.'

'Why?'

'I told that poliswoman we were going in there. To see him.' She releases my hand and looks at me. 'And know what she did?'

'What?'

'She stood right in front of me and shook her head.'

'No way.'

Fuckin' polis cunts.

'Said that if I insisted on doing so then she'd have to arrest me.'

'Arrest *you*, why?'

'Because they said that Mark's body was now a crime scene; that an active murder investigation was now in place, and if anyone tampered with the evidence, they'd be arrested.'

'Fuck sake, man,' I go. Think it's the first time I've sworn in front of her, but I'd no other words.

'My boy's lying dead in a hospital morgue; his name and body being reduced to a bloody crime scene.'

'That's sickening.'

If you'd been there, you'd have battered down every

door in that fuckin' hospital so she could've seen him. You'd have booted that poliswoman in her polis cunt and found out where they were keeping him. How's that for your crime scene? There's no chance you'd have allowed them to be so evil and heartless. Murdered by the Fleeto then murdered again by the polis.

'So the last time I saw our Mark was when he left this house that night. He shouted, "See you later, Mum," at me through the walls. "No messin'," I shouted after him. And those were the final words we said to each other. I got no goodbye from him and he got no goodbye from me.'

You see it all playing out. The poliswoman blocking them from getting into see Biscuit. Mrs McVitie on the floor, being hugged by Denise. The noise they make rushing through the corridors. You've a sudden warmth for Denise now, poor lassie's on the floor cos she'll never see her wee brother again. That's it, finished, finito. OK, so they fought like fuck, but she still loved him. They shared blood, that's why she's on the floor. And see if she wants to get a tattoo, then that's her decision. Some wee prick like me will never stop people feeling what they feel. So stop judging every cunt you meet, you've not got a leg to stand on. You're better than no one, remember that.

'You should make a complaint,' I go.

'That won't bring him back though, will it?' She stands up and hovers over me.

'No, suppose it won't.'

'Know why I'm telling you all of this?'

'Probably cos I'm his mate?'

Was his mate, mate.

'No, Connor, I'm telling you this in case you or any of your daft wee cronies –' she nods to the photo – 'want to carry out some form of revenge for this. I don't want any mother, or in your case, father, to go through what me and our Denise are going through.'

'We're not, I mean, we won't. It's not something we're interested in doing.' She's got her hand on her hip. Clearly the lies are printed all over my face. Thank God Trig isn't here.

'And that goes for the boy who did this ... his parents will be suffering too.'

My face contorts.

'I know,' I go, when what's sitting in my mouth is, *Fuck that wee cunt, he'll be gettin' his soon enough, no danger about that.*

'I want an end to all this violence, you hear me?'

'Aye.'

'I mean it. We're all sick of it.'

You want to confide in her. Go on, unzip your torso and let her see inside. Tell her that you're sick of it as well. Sick to your back fuckin' teeth. Sick of this entire town and the fuckwits who live in it. She'll understand why you hate all this pointless Catholic-Protestant pish. The booze. The lack of . . . everything. Sick that you never get any breaks. Sick of looking at the future version of yourself and all you see is a man on the dole who's sick of life and sick in body. Tell her! She's got a brain, she'll be able to help you.

'Me too. I don't want any violence either, Mrs McVitie.' This bit is true, every ounce of it.

'You're all eighteen now, it's time to grow up and stop all this stupid fuckin' Ned rubbish. You got me?' Denise seems like a chip off the old block. I'd seen Mrs McVitie turn on Biscuit in the blink of an eye loads of times before, I've heard all the fucks and shites and bastards of the day coming out of her mouth, so this isn't a surprise. This is a warning born out of love and anger.

'Aye . . . I mean, yes.'

'You all need to find jobs and start making something of your lives, cut the drinking, cut wandering the streets at night; change your attitudes. Have a bit of pride in yourselves. But no more trouble. You hear me, Connor O'Neill?' Her finger about three inches from my face.

'I do. I do hear you.'

'Cos if you don't, this is where it'll lead to.' She points to Biscuit's empty bed, which I wish I could lie on and pull the covers over my head. It could as well have been a coffin she was pointing to, right enough. I get the message. Loud and clear. I nod my head.

'I know your mum would be saying the same thing to you if she was still here.' Mrs McVitie blesses herself yet again. 'God rest her soul.'

She's hit the bullseye, but Mum would've gone loco. She'd have locked me in my room until she'd found another gaff for us to live in.

'I know she would've,' I go.

'Right, come downstairs,' she goes, walking to the door. 'I've something for you.'

Before heading out, I give his room a final gander. The last time I'll ever set foot in here; I know it. I still see us potting balls on that tiny snooker table, arguing over every shot; playing *Star Wars* with the small cues, or kidding on they were giant joints. Both of them were used in a scrap with the Fleeto when we were sixteen. Mine's rattled off some cunt's napper; his, some cunt's ribcage. No arguing over who won that night. Hate saying it, but he was always much better than me at snooker.

My hand grips the bag like a sack of money. There's a pace in my step. Don't want anyone stopping me for a blether; having to lie at their nosy questions. When I get home it's right up the stairs with it. Under the bed. No . . . behind the wardrobe. No . . . squeezed under the mattress. No . . . oh, for fuck sake. Hard to hide something when you've got nowhere to hide it.

'Here,' Mrs McVitie had said when handing over the bag. 'Don't know why I'm giving you this, but here it is anyway.'

I'd had a quick peek inside then closed it again.

'Sure you don't want to keep hold of it?' I'd gone.

'I can't have that in the house.'

I'd another wee peek.

'But anytime you want it back, it's yours,' I had said. 'I'll make sure I look after it.'

'Well, mibbe that's why I'm giving it to you.'

Denise didn't bother her fat hole getting up to say cheerio. I badly wanted to see Biscuit's name scrawled along her trotters, too. Aw, well. Next time.

'And, Connor?' Mrs McVitie had caught me just before I was leaving. 'Do something positive with your life, son. That's the best way to get your revenge on those who did that to Mark. And the best way to remember him as well.'

Documentary

'That you, Connor?' Dad shouts from the living room. You can tell from the word *That* if he's in rank form or not. Waiting to growl at cunts. 'Get in here now.' Yup, just as I thought. I clutch the bag behind my back and twist my napper around the door.

'What's happening?' I go.

He's on his feet, legs spread, swinging his knackered arms around his body. Sweat's pishin' off him. I'm guessing this is the endgame of four hundred thousand press-ups. A wee cool down. Place smells stuffy, boiled cabbage and sweat. I miss the Glade Mum used to spray, which is saying something cos that would've floored a herd of hippos.

'Where you been?' he asks.

'Just out?'

'Big Seamus Coyle said he saw you standing at Sunnyside this morning.' Two things: one, I'm failing to understand why standing at a train station is a crime? Two, Big Seamus Coyle is a Nobel Prize-winning dick. He's one of Dad's gym sniffers; a verified cock and a half. Ordinarily, I wouldn't believe a word that came out his mouth; man's got more brains in his biceps. 'Going somewhere, were you?'

You want to laugh at him. Point out the fact that you're eighteen and way beyond being escorted on public transport; that the days of needing your dad to hold your pisser are so far in the past that you can't even remember the name of that Dad now. In any case, you don't need the cunt any longer. Reality? You want to tell him that you've recently taken up trainspotting; how you've got a massive hard-on for standing at the far end of rail platforms, jotting train numbers into a notebook. However, knowing that sarcasm and fun has all but disappeared from domestic life, you tell him the truth.

'I went into Glasgow.'

Dad stops stretching his shoulder blades and triceps; shoogles out his arms. His frame becomes rigid. By his expression, you'd honestly think Seamus Coyle had told him I'd been out scoring some brown.

'Glasgow?' he goes, and my head tilts in the same way as a confused dog's. The way he spits Glasgow out you'd think he's talking about Aleppo.

'Aye, Glasgow.'

'Fuck were you doin' in Glasgow?'

His eyes almost hit the ceiling. Must have missed this, but I didn't realise that Glasgow was at the arse end of the world? Mibbe he's raging cos deep down he wanted a dad and son day out. A day of bonding in Argyle Street. Bit of lunch. Cheeky wee pint. Fat fuckin' chance of any of that happening. I glance at their wedding photo by the fireplace. Look at Mum's giant smile and perfect gnashers. His too. It's a fast thought, but I hear the words in my head: *I'm going to make you proud, Mum. Check this out, I was doing some poetry things earlier on today. That's right, poetry.*

'I went into the big bookshop up Sauchiehall Street.'

Look on the cunt's face! Now, if I'd said I'd been to a protein shake drinking competition!

'Bookshop, eh?' His arms drop, his body relaxes. Should've told him that I was on a rampage in George Square; battling with Bridgeton Huns. Just for the rise, you know. 'Up Sauchiehall Street?'

'Aye.'

'Get anything?'

Fuck! Nearly. Flashback. Raging I didn't keep that book now. That would've been me sorted for the night's entertainment.

'Just browsing.' Pretty sure this is the first time we've chatted about books. OK, granted, not in any depth, but still. 'I'm skint.'

His triceps thing kicks-in again.

'Want to know what I think, Connor?'

Erm ... let me have a think about that ... no. But here we fuckin' go. I'm ready. Lob me your best. I can take it all.

'No, what?'

'See, instead of browsing the streets of Glasgow, I think you should be browsing the Job Centre.'

How many times do I need to tell him that everything's online these days? Doesn't matter, he'll never change. Deaf ears. Deaf brain. And, another thing, can you browse the streets? 'Apparently there's jobs galore at the airport, in factories, picking fruit and veg. There're a load of jobs out there. People like you can't be fussy.'

People like me? Fuck does that mean? Thick cunts who leave school, their bags stuffed with a future of fresh air?

'Aye, I'm on it,' I go.

Phone pings. I give it a swatch.

> *Right fannyman doon mine the morra*
> *afternoon time we delt way those fleeto bams*

'Who's that?' Dad goes.

'Just Trig.'

Fuck me, his body's like a spring. Tense relax tense relax. I know he wants to tell me to get rid of Trig, that he's nothing but bad news, that if I keep cutting around with him, I'm either gonna end up in a jail or dead. *He's a horrible wee no-hope, just like his brother and dad* is etched all over his face. Sometimes the eyes have more impact than words. Eyes fuck with your mind; at least you know where you stand with words.

'You goin' out?' he asks.

Is that worry I spy on his chops?

'Don't think so,' I go.

'That Schwarzenegger documentary's on later, if you want to watch it?' he goes, careful to leave out the *with me* bit at the end.

It's not *on*. It's recently been added to Netflix and he's watched it about sixty times already; sitting foaming at all the oiled-up muscles. He wants an answer. I have none. How do you do non-committal? Don't really fancy a night in watching a bunch of men in knickers.

'You not working?' I ask, given that Sunday's one of the maddest nights of the week. The older brigade with cash in their pockets are still rocking about, seeking some final weekend action.

'Night off,' he goes. 'One Sunday a month.'

'Why don't you go out then?' Obviously, I know what his answer is gonna be, something about the competition being just round the corner. But we both know the real reason is more complicated, don't we? Christ, the man's shite scared to go to the shops these days. Thinks people will be talking behind their hands or pointing the finger at him; that everyone thinks he'd been knocking ten lumps of shite out of her. Morning, noon and night. He didn't. I was here. He didn't. Not as much as lifted a pinky. I'd have seen it. And if I'd have seen it, or Mum had told me he'd been knocking her about, I'd have stabbed the cunt in his sleep. No danger. Mean, what man's wife up and does that? Poor cunt's been struggling with that for four years now, and probably for the next four to come. And the four after that. It'll never end.

'Nah, quiet night,' he goes. 'Got to watch what I do for the next couple of weeks anyway.' Points to his body. I'm sure he jiggled his pecks; hate when he does that. Not natural for any human to be doing that. Suddenly I feel sorry for him. Sunday night with no mates. No wife. No son. Just him and Arnold Schwarzenegger. Same as every other night as well.

'I might come down later and watch a bit of it,' I tell him. 'But I'm knackered.'

'Aye, well,' he goes. 'See how you're fixed.' I know he wants to chin me about saying I'm knackered. Rip into me for having the cheek to even consider being knackered. Holding it in is killing him. Eyes, you see, all in them eyes!

And that's it. Bonding session over. But it's something. Got to hold onto all those somethings. Big or small.

The bag rustles in my hand. I don't squeeze it too much cos it's actually making me feel a bit uncomfortable. Can't imagine looking at it, never mind touching it. And now it's found a new home: my room. Jammed down the back of my bed, right at the corner of the wall. The great hope is that I'll go to sleep, dream of something calm, wake up and forget that I ever put it there. Try to forget that Mrs McVitie gave me to reach over and yank her tongue right out her mouth. She didn't have a scooby – good listener though, and quite good-looking – she tried to slice your brain open and figure out what was going on inside. The whole shebang was joyless, pointless pish. Thing is, that counsellor didn't see how you were far too weak to lift her weight away from the rope's tension, or how you stood frozen, petrified to go near her. She didn't know how stiff she was. The woman said that you were far too young to understand or make sense of what was going on. But it wasn't that, was it? No. It was something you didn't tell anyone about: your voice wouldn't work, you opened your mouth but nothing came out. Too mute to scream. The noise of it might've helped, someone might've come … you'll never know, right? Time after time, you've told yourself that it wouldn't have mattered anyway, every cunt screams around here, yours would've only blended in with the others. No one would've given a fuck; probably told you to rap it, *Keep that fuckin' racket down.* Silent screams still haunt you to this day. You hear them everywhere. Ears are battered by them. From that day on, your dad looked at you differently cos you didn't scream. Cos you didn't raise the alarm. Cos you failed to save her. Aye, that's right, it was you who made the noose, you who slung it around her neck, you who hoisted her up. You who killed her. That'll be fuckin' right. From then to now, any hint of happiness was sucked from every wall, ceiling and floor in your gaff. A giant grey make me special either, cos I know I'm not alone in this world. Although sometimes I think that people like us are always alone in this world. Hidden away and stuck inside our Treacle Towns. Unequal and unrecognised. Driftwood floating down our manky canal; surviving day to day, unable to plan for anything or get excited about the future. No pleasure. No prospects. And what's a life without pleasure or prospects? Big question, that one ... but I'll tell you what I think it is: it's like living in a vast open prison where everyone *is* screaming but no cunt's listening. If, on the rare occasion, they do manage to hear us, all they do is stare through the perimeter fence, totally unmoved, as if we're animals in the concrete zoo. Oh, they're more than happy for us to stab each other to death and obliterate the place, no danger about that. Cos to them, that's what animals do, isn't it? And that's all we are to them. Actually, much more. We're the murderers, the racists, the bigots, the abusers, the swindlers, the criminals, the junkies, the alkies, the scroungers ... the very reason why this country's a cesspit. We're to blame. All our fault. Us. Not them. Us. So don't get too upset when we don't *confide in friends*, cos the reality is we're all busy putting one foot in front of the other and trying to find nuggets of peace. No space to be telling our mates how we feel. Anyway, they all know cos we're all feeling the same fuckin' thing. It's called existing. Is it any wonder some people believe that slinging a rope around their neck and swinging from the rafters is a better option than just existing? Come on, bet if we *confide in friends* you'll find that we've all thought about it … at least once a day.

No cunt is running to help. No one ever comes. Treacle Town in a nutshell.

My dream isn't calm. It's never calm, especially when she arrives.

Are you there, son?

I'm here.

I need you to come with me.

I don't want to.

Don't be scared, I'll protect you.

I can't move.

I need you to understand.

You don't have to explain.

I do, sweetheart.

I tried to stop it.

There's nothing you could've stopped, Connor.

There was, I was weak. I could've stopped it days or months before.

That's kind, but it wasn't possible.

It's how I feel.

You're kind.

I miss you.

Kindness suits you.

Brick

'Up the stairs,' Sean nods, as he stands aside to let me in. I can't remember a time when he said something normal to me, like *Awright, wee man?* or *What's the craic, Con?* After Mum died all he could muster was, *If ye ever need any hash, geez a shout?* Followed by a wink. Think the offer's been pulled now.

'Awright, Sean?' I go, brushing past him. He's got the body of a middleweight and the neck of a heavyweight. Solid enough. He might be as hard as Tarzan's feet but he's taken a good few second prizes in his time. Hard to remember him without swollen eyes. For someone who hovers between handsome and right ugly cunt, he gets his fair share of women.

'Naw, am no,' he goes. 'Tell that wee prick he better get his shit together and do somethin'.'

'About what?'

'Those orange bastards that done Biscuit.' He nods his head towards the top of the stairs. 'Yeez need to sort them out; get the next dig in. Know what I mean?'

'Aye,' is all I can muster.

'Get that lezzy Nails to throw some shapes.'

He makes some slashing kung fu moves in front of my face. Supposed to be taekwondo, but he comes across as a right fud. Mainly cos he is.

I want to smack the head on that coked-up nose of his. Put more swelling onto his face. Although it's probably the longest conversation he's ever had with me since I started knocking around with Trig. Before I get a chance to answer, he pulls a single-skinner joint from behind his ear, sticks it in his mouth, shakes his head despairingly and fucks off to the living room.

The carpet that runs up the stairs is so bare it almost looks like a layer of leather. Some patterned monstrosity from the eighties. The only word I'd use to describe Trig's house is mingin'. Rentokil would think twice. All our houses have some level of ming about them I suppose, but Trig's is a cut above.

'Aw, there he is!' Trig goes when I enter. Smell of green in the air. Wee Z gives me a thumbs up, he's slouched on the bed, bleamed out his box.

'Hit me,' Nails goes, holding up her palm for me to slap, which I do. She's the only one who's not stoned. Not her bag. Athlete.

'Fuck is that?' I ask Trig, who's standing walloping some cosh contraption against his hand. A weapon made of paper.

'This?' He holds it up. Offers it. I take it, examine it. Tap it against the side of my head. Harder. Harder.

'Fuckin' hell, some dunt off that, isn't there?' I hand it back to him.

'One smack of this will split those Fleeto cunts' heads wide open.' Trig whacks the weapon down on the bed, Wee Z comes alive. I glance at Nails, she flicks her brows.

'What even is that thing?' she asks.

'It's called a Millwall brick,' Trig goes. 'Our Sean made it for me. It's basically a newspaper rolled up and folded into itself; the folded bit is as solid as a rock. Whoever invented it is a fuckin' genius in my book.'

'All a bit *Blue Peter*, if you ask me,' Nails goes.

'Aye, well, two rapid with this and Peter would turn from blue to red.' He spanks the bed again. Twice.

'Gonna no do that?' Wee Z goes.

'And know the best bit?' Trig raises it up with two hands. 'It's a newspaper, so the polis can do fuck all about it.'

'Genius,' Nails goes. I smell the sarcasm in her voice, she's trying to hide it, but her tone's a giveaway.

'Our Sean said that all those mad Millwall casuals used to battle with them back in the day.'

Now Wee Z looks up with a confused glance. His eyes shift between mine and Nails's. I'm shifting between Wee Z's and Nails's. It's like that scene in *Reservoir Dogs* without the guns. The pair of them are clearly waiting for me to say something. We're all thinking the same thing. I know it. Trig's face looks as if he's lost a fiver and found a tenner. Guy's ecstatic with the idea of knocking some cunt's pan in with a folded piece of newspaper.

Fuck this, I'm saying it: 'Trig, you really want us to battle the Fleeto with a bunch of newspapers?'

'Aye.'

I glare at the other two, hoping for some sort of backup. Nothing.

'Really?' I shake my head; mostly at Nails and Wee Z. 'That's mental.'

'Con, this is a proper weapon, son.' Trig glares at me and runs his tongue over his yellow teeth. 'But if you've got yer knob in a twist, then let's hear it.'

You really need the other two to step up, to help you out, to see what's raging inside you. You're shit-scared and you need them to see that. You know they're feeling the same. You know it! You've entered into a room full of that bullshit and bravado; not a fuckin' truthful sentiment to be seen, let alone aired. Come on, admit it, you shower of fuckwits, admit that *we're all terrified*. Admit that images of Biscuit lying dead in his coffin are flashing through your minds at this moment. Admit that you don't want your heart stabbed. Admit it all. You'll have me right behind you. But they don't say a word. You're all making stupid fuckin' eye movements at each other, like you did when you huddled around someone's phone

147

watching those first grainy porn clips. Awkward and terrified. And the get out? Act as if you couldn't give two fucks. Everybody thinking they're Billy Big Bawz. Nothing phases nobody. Call it super-charged peer pressure. So, to get this straight, you're all just gonna say heehaw, risk everything, to save your fuckin' face? Mean, it's beyond fuckwittery, isn't it?

Sometimes you wish these spanners weren't your mates. PaulaTik and Ginger Archie jump into your mind for some reason; think they're planning a kamikaze outing with their mates? Not a chance, their heads are full of words and creativity, and hopes for the future.

'The four of us can't just go up there,' Wee Z goes. 'We'll get leathered.' *Finally* someone shows a bit of courage.

'Not if we use our noggins,' Trig goes. 'Keep our wits about us.'

'Noggins? That's us lot fucked, then,' Nails goes, trying to cut the fear with a joke.

Trig grips the Millwall brick tighter. You'd swear he's desperate to get going this very minute. Mibbe the other two are as well, it's hard to know what anyone's thinking.

You feel distant from them; as if you're hiding something. You think how they don't know you at all, they'll never really know who you are. Apart from bolting – mibbe running all the way into Glasgow and giving that poetry workshop another blast – all you want to do is sit down and smoke a joint. Forget yourself for a while. Be in Wee Z's land. Think of a world that brings only peace and quiet. Dunno, the stuff that Ginger Archie, PaulaTik and Vicky Rooney think about in the dead of night: poems, art, music. That's harmless enough, isn't it? That's the kinda stuff that won't get you sent to jail or the morgue; those things'll bring wealth to your soul. But you're not like those people, are you? Your mind's consumed with revenge, death and football. And the rest. Is it a wonder your head lives in a constant grinder? You remember one time you stared out of your bedroom window and watched the wind howling through the trees; you remember how stunning that sight was: a gaggle of green branches dancing away the day and loving life. You also remember how sad you were, cos those trees made you jealous of their joy. You closed the blinds to save yourself; you didn't want those trees laughing at the trapped boy in the window. And you're still trapped; standing here in this kip of a bedroom, hand rooted down your trackie bottoms, trapped in their friendships, trapped in the ongoing nightmare. And, unless you put a stop to this illness, you'll be forever stuck.

'Just as long as we get that murdering Hun bastard, Yobboy,' Trig goes. 'That'll do.' Again the bed takes the force of the Millwall brick. Again Wee Z shites himself. 'What do you say, Con?' Trig stares at me, so do the others. Who the fuck made me their leader?

This is my opportunity. Grab it. I hear the words I want to speak. My jaw loosens and mouth opens, my lips make an odd shape. They're all waiting on this stuttering eejit. I'm about to say something, but I can't. My mouth slowly closes again. Well grabbed, Con.

'Con, you've done that diss,' Nails pipes up, which tells me she's on my wavelength. 'Haven't you?'

I say nothing.

'That's right, aye,' Wee Z goes.

So, we're all agreed then, none of us are up for this.

'Fuck that,' Trig spits. 'I already told him that a diss is as useful as drinking piss water.' I nod my head in agreement with Trig and suddenly feel as if I'm letting the other two down. Disappointment seeps from their eyes. I was their saviour, their route out and now I've bawzed it up for them. Is there any cunt in this life who's not disappointed with me? The Millwall brick gets held up like a trophy. 'Our Sean showed me how to make this, so I can do one for each of us.'

I want to tell him to shove it right up his arse. And that of his wanker of a brother. The anger's rising, short breaths in and out. I want to slag the fuck out of his green, white and gold walls. Mean, that takes a special kinda nuts to do that. Not even proper Irish. Wannabes. Same as most people around here. Obsessed with everything and anything Irish. Tried to get my head around that, sang the Rebel songs, chanted the IRA slogans, but never got it, or believed it. Fuckin' red neck, doing that now.

'What's the big plan then?' Nails goes. I fire her a dagger. Wee Z's face is a picture of worry. *It's OK, wee man, it'll be all OK. Try not to worry. Someone will look after yer mum and dad if it goes tits up.* And it will. No danger.

Trig starts pacing the room. Shifting the Millwall brick from one hand to another. Daft cunt couldn't spell 'plan'; he's making it up as we're looking at him. Tell you what, we're some spangles for letting ourselves be led by this fuckin' loola. Someone's needing to have a word with us.

'Best day is a Sunday,' Trig goes. 'They'll be fucked after the weekend, their guard'll be down.' He tips his Burberry hat with the Millwall brick, then rubs hard at the back of his head. 'We'll definitely get one of them stoating about on their own.' He stops pacing and looks at us in turn, you can tell his head's already well and truly inside the battle. Points the Millwall brick at us. I'm just waiting on him shouting *This is a stick up!* 'I don't care who gets it, as long as some bam's getting it, know what I mean?'

Oh, we know what you mean, we just don't agree with it.

'Aye,' Nails goes.

'Aye,' so does Wee Z.

Again, six eyes on me. Eight, if you include Biscuit's, which I don't.

'It's what Biscuit would want us to do, Con,' Trig goes.

The skin around your cheeks is as tight as the leather on your one-tens; happens to your face when the eyes form into a couple of raging slits. Something in you wants to grab that Millwall brick and wrap it around his skull. Ragdoll the cunt all over the room until he stops speaking. And hopefully breathing. Then you remember one of her lines: *I want an end to all this violence, you hear me?* When will her words leave you? Probably never.

How the fuck does he know what Biscuit would've wanted you to do? Fact: Biscuit thought Trig was the thickest prick he knew, bright as a power cut. Biscuit couldn't be doing with him. Fact: he was gonna boot their friendship into touch after the summer. Trig dragged him, and everyone else, down. Biscuit wasn't after the world. A wee job that could've taken him somewhere; decent pay, proper clobber. You two used to joke, say Trig was gonna graduate from being a street arse to holding up the bookies one day. You've no intention of being his wingman.

'You sure about that?' I go.

'What?'

'About Biscuit wanting us to do it?'

'Hunner per cent,' Trig goes. Glares at me. Stares at the others. 'Meet here, Sunday at twelve.' Nails and Wee Z don't react. 'In and out, bish bash. We'll go and get pished afterwards. Mad Dog's on me.'

'Bish bash, magic,' I mutter to myself.

'What was that, Con?' he goes.

'Nothin', talkin' to myself.'

'Aye, thought so.'

Swear to fuck, he twists his hand around that paper weapon, gripping it hard. I clock his movement and he clocks that I've clocked it. Is he fuckin' serious? Is he actually threatening me? In his own gaff? Acting the fuckin' honcho cos his dick brother's downstairs. He knows if I was to ever make a move on him, Sean would be up here in a flash; any excuse for that maniac to get the fists out. Apples don't fall far from the tree in this house, do they? I wasn't gonna do this, but I think it's time for me to pull out my own version of a Millwall brick.

'I spoke to Biscuit's mum the other day,' I go. He doesn't even flinch.

'How was she?' Wee Z asks.

'Tickety-boo, Z,' Nails spits. 'How the fuck you think she was?'

'Awright. Awright. Just asking.'

Wee Z sinks back into the bed.

'And?' Trig goes, eyes still glued to me, coshed-up, ready to make his move.

'And she said that she doesn't want any more trouble,' I go.

Is that a who-gives-a-fuck chuckle he's just done?

'That right?' It's as if Trig's in a monotone trance now.

'Aye, that's right,' I go.

'That's what she said?'

'Can't remember the exact words, Trig.'

'That's what she said about her murdered son, did she?'

'She made it clear that she doesn't want any more violence.' I feel my body moving closer, almost toe to toe. 'No more blood. No more poor cunts losing their children. Know what I mean?' Nails and Wee Z start nodding their heads like dashboard dolls. Delighted that I've saved them from whatever carnage was coming.

'Defo agree with that, man,' Wee Z adds.

'Shut the fuck up, you!' Trig growls at him.

'Simmer down, Trig,' Nails goes. I'm convinced she gets in just before he can spout some racist shit. He's definitely got it in him, so I wouldn't put it past the cunt. Nails stiffens her shoulders. Not the first time she's come to Wee Z's aid. If ever a person hated a bully, it's our Nails. I know who my money would be on if it came to it.

'Aye, whatever, Nails,' Trig goes, then starts doing his pacing and thinking action again. I need to leave. The green, white and gold walls are beginning to wreck my head. Stomach's back in its blender. Blood icing up. Just breathe, Con. In through the nose. Wim Hof's all over you. But the only breathing I can hear is coming from Trig's mouth; guy's overflowing with adrenalin. Cosh tapping hard against his knee.

I close my eyes for a nanosecond. She appears:

I'm here, son.

Are you, though?

I've never left. I'd never do that.

But that's exactly what you've done.

It's complicated, but I can show you what I mean.

I don't want to see.

This place isn't safe, you need to come with me now.

I can't.

You've nothing to be afraid of.

I'm stuck.

I can help you.

How can you help me, when you couldn't help yourself?

I'm sorry for creating a mess, sweetheart. Really, I am.

Well, the biggest mess of them all is staring right at you.

Just walk out. Walk away. Leave. I did.

It's not that easy.

It is. Come. I'll show you.

'Naw, I'm no buying that, Con,' Trig goes.

'Buying what?'

'That her son's been murdered down her local park and she doesn't want any revenge?' The knee tapping gets more vigorous, more violent; hope his kneecap smashes into a million pieces. 'No. Not buyin' that, Con.'

'Not asking you to buy it, but just know it's true. I was actually in Biscuit's room when she told me that.'

'His bedroom?' Wee Z asks.

'Aye.'

155

'Cool.'

We all glare at Wee Z.

'What?' he goes.

'So, what would you suggest we do, Con?' Trig asks. 'What's your great plan? Write a fuckin' song?'

I rub my face, try to take the sting out of my eyes. Must be the lingering smoke. I face him up. Stand my ground.

'How about we just do nothing, Trig?'

He laughs, thinks I'm joking. This isn't the Con O'Neill he knows and loves ... sometimes hates. Then it arrives, the realisation that I'm deadly serious; the contortion on his coupon is hilarious to watch. What I've suggested has confused the fuck out of him.

'Eh?'

'How about we just do nothing?'

'Do nothing? Like, *nothing*?'

'Live our lives, forget about the Fleeto. Get on with life and remember the good things about Biscuit. Surely doin' the best we can for him and his mum is the best revenge there is?'

Trig shakes his head and sniggers.

'You're takin' the piss, Con. I know you.'

'I'm not. I'm serious.'

'Naw, you're fuckin' at it, son.'

I turn to face Nails and Wee Z.

'What do you two think?'

Wee Z's too scared to answer in case Trig scuds him with

156

that Millwall brick. Nails just shrugs, she's so laid-back sometimes that you'd think she was horizontal. I'm beginning to think she's been on that green after all.

'I'm easy,' she goes.

I'm easy? Clearly she doesn't grasp the scale of this shit. Here's me offering her the opportunity of not getting her head spattered all over Fleeto territory and she's giving it *I'm easy* and shrugging her fuckin' shoulders. I give up.

'For fuck sake, Nails,' I go.

Trig's got a smug look on his chops. He fires the Millwall brick towards Nails, who grabs it one-handed.

'There you go,' he goes. 'Everyone else is well up for it.' Think Wee Z is about to start crying. *Fuckin' speak-up, man!* 'Right, so, Sunday here. Twelve bells.'

There's nothing else you can do. You're exhausted with trying to talk some sense into them. They're lost causes, destined to be in this town for an eternity. Prison, smack, dole, misery. You're surprised at Nails. Fear for Wee Z. If you can't save them, then save yourself. It's not their fault they can't see what's in front of them. The possibilities. They've left you with no choice, you've got to fly solo, Con; got to kickstart those dreams, create your own future. You look at them in turn, thinking it might be the last time you see them, at least in this state. You've no more words. Words are useless. What are words without actions attached? A pile of pish, that's what.

'Fuck this, I'm out of here,' I go.

I'm not even halfway down the leather stairs when Trig shouts after me.

'Sunday. Twelve bells. Don't be fuckin' late.' I don't say anything or look back. Never look back. 'And none of this *let's do nothing* pish again. We know you're good at that.'

I stop. Look back.

'Fuck's that supposed to mean?' I go.

'Think you know, Con.'

I'm about to run back up the stairs and header his mouth. Shut the cunt up forever.

'No, I don't know. You tell me.'

He takes one step down.

I take one step up without realising that I'm at a disadvantage. One boot and I'm tumbling.

'Fuck you on about, Trig, eh?'

'If you say or do nothing, then people get fucked, don't they?' His voice is cold. An ugly, spiteful cunt of a voice. If this was anyone else, anyone with brain cells, I'd be sure they were nodding towards Mum, but it's Trig we're talking about here, he's too thick to make the connection. But, then again, he might be. Prick!

Two options: run and hammer the prick, or bolt.

I make sure I slam the door as hard as I can, just to get right on Sean's tits. Hopefully he'll take it out on his wee brother.

Tickets

Hi Connor,
We'd be delighted to welcome you to our Scottish Youth Poetry Group. Our doors are open for everyone and anyone, regardless of circumstances and/or level of 'slam' experience. We meet every Sunday morning at 10 a.m. at the Royal Conservatoire of Scotland in Glasgow. Do send me an email if you want to come join us.

Best,
Vicky
(If you have something to read to the group, do bring it along. If not, then that's perfectly fine.)

I have to read the email about six times cos my concentration is all over the shop. I'm still fuckin' bealing at Trig and his desire to burst people. He's hiding behind the idea of getting revenge; in my opinion, that's just his excuse for being nothing short of a crazy cunt. My heart won't stop racing. Brain is on an axis. Can't think of much else. Need to calm down. In the past when we were battle-planning, my adrenalin would fill me with a rush of excitement that whizzed around my body like an F1 car. I'd visualise smashing my fists and feet off whoever got in the way of them, see blood splattered over my white trainers, hear the troops' celebration during the post-battle swally session. But now, if I try to visualise those things, I'd almost want to puke my guts up.

For the first time in yonks I want my dad, not for hugs or anything like that, just to be in his company. For us to be flooting about in the same space. I'd even be prepared to snaffle into his bland scran and watch that *Pumping Iron* documentary. We might even get a few laughs in; could spot him when he's lifting. I scroll through my phone until I get to his number; change the name I've given him, so *Muscles* now becomes *Dad*. Better. Accurate. No need to play the clown any more; time to box that prick and lock him away for all time. I stare at my phone for ages, more scrolling. Change *Mammy* to *Mum. Biscuit* becomes *Mark (Biscuit) McVitie*. Wonder what happens to these numbers when they're no longer needed or in use. Mean, is there a huge graveyard for all the dead numbers somewhere? Do they float around in the air for eternity? Nowhere to go, no one to speak to. Purposeless. One day they're full of value, and the next, a giant fuck all. I press Mum's number and place the phone to my ear. Dead. Do the same with Biscuit's. His is still alive:

160

Awright, you've reached the top kiddie's phone. Leave a message. If I don't like you, you'll get no reply, if I do, you'll get a text if I'm feeling generous. Right, hit me. His number's yet to be defunct. I've recorded his voice message onto my phone so he'll never be defunct. And that's it. That's all I'll have from him until my number rises up to meet his. More scrolling.

Message Nails:

> *We need to do something about that crazy cunt*

Nails pings back:

> *U no wot hes like*

> *Aye, but this is another level*

> *We cant do nuthin Con bout Biscuit*

> *U still there?*

> *No, back at my gaff*

> *K. Witz happenin?*

Usual, da being a da.
Same dick different
day

                    As per

Better go. Training
in a bit

                    Seriously, have a word
                    with Trig

I'll need to do a solo mission on Nails; go see her soon, try and talk sense into her skull. Make her see what she could be missing out on if she allows Trig to thrust a Millwall brick into her hand. I'll talk about the Olympics. The Commonwealth Games. *These* are the places where she should be booting fuck out of people, not in some clatty dogshit-filled park in the arse end of Arseville. If there's anyone among us with a massive opportunity to get the fuck out of here, it's her.

It hits me after the seventh time of reading that email. Sunday could be one eventful day. Bit of slam poetry in the morning, slam some cunt with a Millwall brick in the afternoon, then slam a bottle of Mad Dog into me at night. Sounds like a belter. Living the best life.

At the bottom of the email Vicky put links up to another two poems. I click. Some guy, ages with me, stands at the mic. Why the fuck do they all need a mic? Jeans ripped at the knees, Converse. Baggy T-shirt. Dripping in cheap gold. Hair shaved to the scalp. Neck tat. Could be a Halloween version of Eminem. His voice sounds nothing like ours. Bit of a posh lassie's voice; putts from the rough, I'd wager. No name on the geezer? He leans into the mic and goes, *This is a poem about my ex-boyfriend.* Told you! I should be a polisman . . . I shouldn't . . . but, you know, I've an eye for things. *So, here's to you,* he goes, all angry as fuck, pointing directly at the camera. *And you know who you are. It's called 'Losing the Will to Live'.* He does a camp twist of his head, like that Italian spanner from *Strictly* does. Mum loved that show. When yer man looks straight into the camera again, his expression changes. He seems sad, hurt, damaged. His face reminds me of Wee Z's when he's scared, different colour but similar vulnerability. It's as if yer man's de-aged himself and reverted back to being a wean. I shuffle on the chair and decide that this skinhead geezer's ex-boyfriend needs a right hard boot in the stones.

> I'm losing the will to live when I'm around you.
> Not that I wish to die, simply not to live.
> To inhabit your time, your world,
> the place where the things you only you only you
> understand or happen or make sense.

I'm senseless when I'm with you.
Jesus!
Even now,
right now,
saying these words,
these very words,
that last word there:
WORD! THERE!
WHATEVER!
Even now,
standing here,
scratching at these memories,
sweating,
hoping that I can escape your fog.
But there's no hope of that
with you here, always
near.
I'm losing the will to live.

You see
there ain't no love in my world,
ain't no happiness
and you're making it worse;
A curse.
It's hanging around my neck
like the weight of what?

A wet welly.
Even now I can feel it,
I can feel it even now.
Pulling me
down down a damp
well.
Into the land of wet welly hell.

You see,
there ain't no love any more.
Ain't no love out there.
Nobody's sharing anything.
Self-preservation the new foundation
of personal advancement and inner peace.
But you *still* refuse to give my head peace.
Love?
Don't talk to me.
You rabbit on about
uni costs, publishing jobs, LGBTQI-plus and the rest.
Enough!

There ain't no love in the world.
The world's gone ballistic,
bonkers,
cracking up
on buckled knees.

Subliminally
we're told we should live in fear.
But how can I live in fear if you're still here?
Near.
Chewing at my ear about:
Food bank invasion
Illegal occupation
Rogue states
Podcasts
Covid
Anti-vax fuckers
Emission gas
Wind farms
Religious zealots
Conceptual artists
Yes/No
Time for change
In/Out
Levelling up
MPs
PMs
Milking the gravy train
Right wing
Left wing
Stealing every fucking grain
of your hatred.

You never asked, I fear them all, too.

But,
I'll need you with me if they decide to call.
You see
I'm losing the will to live
with the thought of you *not* being around.
Not that I'd wish to die, simply not to live.
I'll try and inhabit your time, your world,
the place where the things you only you only you
understand or happen or make sense.
I'd be senseless without you.
Jesus!
Even now,
right now,
spouting these words,
these very words,
that last word there:
WORD! THERE!
WHATEVER!
Even now
standing here
scratching at these memories,
sweating,
hoping that your fog will shroud me.
There's simply no hope

with you *not* here, *not* near.

I'm losing the will to live.

Anyway,

How are things with you?

Mean, how can I bring something to the group when this is the kinda stuff they're churning out? I'd get laughed out of town if I ever read the rants that were swirling around inside my head. Or the words I've already written over the years. Things I could write about Trig at this moment could fill a book. And not one compliment among them. The word 'cunt' crops up regularly, it has to be said. The Mum stuff could fill a library.

Suddenly thinking it's a world that you definitely belong to, you go get your notebook and grab a pen. You find a blank page and stare at the white nothingness of it. Do you actually belong, you wonder? Well, do you? You tap the pen against your teeth. If you really think you don't belong, or you're not wanted, then it's a slap in the puss to everyone else around here who are made to believe the same thing. On a daily basis. Come on, someone's got to lead the way, to give the rest of the deadbeats in this town some sort of hope. Fuck sake, there's an opportunity out there. Grab it and show them how much you do belong. You grip your pen firmly in your hand and scribble down a title. You look at it, let it rest in your mind. You know what you want to say, and how to say it, but writing it down is a different matter. You shake your head at the title. Is that title a cliché of your people? *Your* people! What does that even mean? You consider, but fail to scrub it out. Why is that? You slam the notebook shut.

I open Vicky's email again.

Dear Vicky,
Thanks for sending me details about the Scottish Youth Poetry Group. I would like to attend on Sunday, but I don't have much experience, so I might not bring anything to read. Is that OK?

Sincerely,
Connor O'Neill

As soon as you click the send button you instantly regret it; wish you could dive inside the computer and rub out the Internet. But what's the worst that can happen if you don't attend? They're hardly gonna send out a tooled-up poetry mob to recite you to death, are they? No, the worst that'll happen is that you'll feel the need to always remain in your box; you'll never make an attempt to step out of your (dis) comfort zone. You'll spend a lifetime with a chip (sack of tatties) on both shoulders, complaining about how people like you (us) haven't had any breaks in life. Deep down, you'll know how you turned your back on the breaks that did come your way. When you're fifty, sixty, seventy and facing death, you'll have a lifetime of regrets to look back on.

I open my notebook again. Hammer out a first line. Then a second. A third doesn't come as quick cos I just can't seem to get that spangle Trig out of my mind. No use fighting it, he has to get ten lumps of shite knocked out of him. Pen and paper only. No fists. No kicks. No blood. Done with that. I search for a third line. Think. Think. Think.

I lob the notebook on my bed – this slam lark isn't easy. I should put on Killer Mike or Wu-Tang in the hope of generating some inspiration, but I don't bother – I open the second link that Vicky sent instead. Watching these videos gives me more these days than rap and hip-hop. Makes me want to be part of something positive; a group intent on running mouths instead of amok. The next video comes alive. HEY! It's only one of the numpties who was on the train last week. Wearing the exact same Stone Island gear. Must have filmed it the day I bottled it. Again, no name given. He looks like a Josh or a Jake or a Prick. I watch with a *Right, dickbawz, show me what you've got* expression on my face. I know the drill at this stage: pause a wee bit, compose yourself, let the tongue wag. And when it does, when he starts slamming, this dude smacks me with a killer first line. Note to self: get them on the edge of their seats with a banging opening. My arse teeters on the edge of mine.

Do you know what I really hate?

As well as Tories in elected seats
and the rise of the Right on our streets?

As well as ignorant twats who believe
threats come from countries
ending in -AN or
from the devout who read the Koran?

As well as Fascism, Nepotism,
Imperialism,
Capitalism, Sexism, Sectarianism,
and all other invented -ISMS?

As well as those who sing about a land
                    of free and brave
who now hang their flag
where they once hung their slave?

That's what I really hate.

BUT APART FROM ALL THAT.

Do you know what really gets on my nerves?
Tacky tattoos that adorn the skin of loutish twats:

Footballers and their followers.
These post-modern culture-vulture scavengers
know the score,
know the script.
Each one an urban prophet.

Instant inspiration at the twitch of an eye,
life's summation on perpetual supply.
Immediate motivation direct
from the mouths of
Cristiano, Mandela, Hitler, Mao, Marx, Messi or Plato.

Roman numerals:
an eternal reminder of
Weddings, Births, Funerals.
Moralistic proverbs weighed down with edifying gravitas
in every language
for today's Boss-wearing badass.

The evidence is there for all to see:
Every saint has a past, every sinner has a future.
I sin but I'm not the devil.
Only Jesus can judge me.

Really?
I think we'll be the judge of that.

'I hereby sentence you to life in prison
for acts against humanity and common decency!'

Where's your Jesus now,
ya tattoo-wearing dickhead clown?

That's what really gets on my nerves.

BUT APART FROM ALL THAT.

Do you know what really *really* gets on my tits?

Those sharp suit-wearing pricks
who
go on and on about their precious profession
until they finally focus on you . . . as a wee
                              afterthought . . .
voice full of condescension,
and ask:
'What is it you do yourself?'
Or worse:
'And what do you make?'
And I take a deep breath, compose myself, and I say:
'What do I make?
'I make folk like you feel unhappy about your existence
'I make folk like you want to pick up a book

173

'I make folk like you question their validity

'I make folk like you crave some humility.

'I tell people if you want to lead life decently you have
to use this –'

(Guy points to his head.)

'And if you look into this –'

(Guy points to his heart.)

'You'll realise that someone who judges you
for the job you do for the money you make
should be given this –'

(Guy holds up his middle finger.)

'That's what I make.'

And I'll *gladly* tell *you*
what I do?

I define someone by the person
and not the profession
I don't bow my head to an inflated bank balance
an overrated suit

an overstated ego

or a job of repute.

I search for what's inside someone

because that's what I think is true.

I try to make a difference.

Now what about you?

BUT APART FROM ALL THAT.

Do you know what *really really* rattles my cage?

Slam poets who don't know when to get off the stage.

Now I'm cursing myself for not waltzing into the Royal Conservatoire of Scotland and having a blether with this guy. I've a hate list as long as the River Clyde; make your eyes water, so it would. We could've exchanged lists. I could've told him all about this town, spewed my soul about Mum, Biscuit and life. But, seriously, no joke, if I'd been watching this geezer live, I'd have hopped off my seat and applauded the fuck out of that. I'm half-thinking of sharing the link with the troops, along with PaulaTik and Ginger Archie's poems. No doubt they'd try and rip the pish out of them, but if they'd give it a chance, give it a solid listen, they'd be blown away. Like me. Bet they would.

Right, I'm well up for this, ready to be heard, ready to let them hear the voice of Connor O'Neill. Knowing exactly what I want to say, I grab my notebook and start with this:

> *Waiting in the chippy queue*
> *They fire their daggers at you:*

I'm just about to rattle down a few more lines when his voice bellows from below.

'Connor!'

You just know from the tone that all's not well. Obviously my instinct is to jump to thinking about that bellend Trig. What's Dad heard? What does he know? He always has his ear to the ground. If that walloper, Sean, has said anything about what he thinks he does and doesn't know, then I'll fuckin' shop him to the polis for punting coke around the schemes. And pish coke into the bargain. Aye, he thinks no cunt knows, but I've got news for him. Well, obviously I won't shop him, cos I don't want to visit the hospital, but the fear Dad's voice triggers in me shatters my nerves.

'Connor!' he shouts again.

That'll be the slam done for the day then.

'Aye?' I shout back at him.

'Get down here now.'

He's standing in the middle of the living room juggling a tub of bronzing cream. Tossing it between his hands as if it was a hot tattie. You're fuckin' shittin' me, man, if you think

I'm applying that on to your plums. My hands aren't going anywhere near his skin. Good thing is, he doesn't seem off his nut with rage. Feels good to be in the clear, even though I've done nothing wrong.

'What are you up to?' he goes, accusation written all over his coupon. Shite, mibbe I'm not in the clear, he must've spied me watching the slam poems online; he's gonna go through me for that. A tenner other parents would be out buying up stacks of poetry books if they discovered their kids had a keen interest in the art. Mine? Well, he wants to tear me a new arsehole and ridicule the fuck out of me. I hit panic-station mode and formulate all my excuses.

'Nothing, just fannying about.' Honest to fuck, is that the best I can come up with? 'Trying to look for jobs actually.' Better. Much better. He'll love that; it'll put him off all scent.

His eyes widen.

'Aye?'

'Aye.'

'Any luck?'

'Time Capsule are looking for lifeguards,' I tell him. 'Fourteen quid an hour.'

He flips the bronzing cream up in the air, loops once. He catches it again. All without taking his eyes off me. Impressive, credit where credit's due. Think my mention of the Time Capsule has catapulted him back to happier times. He loved taking me there. At least I think he did.

'Do you not need a lifeguarding certificate for that?'

'Aye, but I think they put you through the course,' I go. I only know this cos Nails's big cousin works there. Makes a fortune. He told me to apply. I'll give it serious consideration. Plus, I'm a half-decent swimmer. I could do twenty lengths without stopping, no bother at all.

'Sounds good, did you apply?'

'No yet, but I will.'

I'll apply for the shits and giggles. He throws the bronzing cream up again. Goes for a double loop this time. Still with his eyes fixed on me. Crashes to the ground. Some eejits just don't know when to quit when they're ahead. Got to hand it to him.

'I'm no putting that on for you,' I go, as he's bending down to retrieve it. 'If that's what you're after.'

'I wouldn't ask you,' he sniggers. 'You wouldn't know how to do it properly.' If ever there was a time to be delighted at being pig ignorant about something. 'Big Linda usually does it for me anyway.'

Big Linda did Mum's hair and nails. A top-notch beauty expert by all accounts, which is ironic given her size and love of Pringles. Telling you, that woman could suck one of those tubes empty in under ten seconds. She's got the job of bronzing up my dad before he enters the competition of muscles. Rather her than me.

'Smashing,' I go.

He places the cream on the mantelpiece and smiles.

'Time Capsule, eh?' he goes.

I know why he's smiling, the Time Capsule is one of the few happy places in our memories. I remember going down the flumes in his lap when I was a wean, both of us screaming our heads off, the closest and cheapest thing this town has to a rollercoaster. Him teaching me how to swim there, breaststroke and front crawl. I remember him showing me how to dive, how to hold my breath under water for more than twenty seconds and how to ride the wave machine. We used to team up to splash Mum, the pair of us working together to tsunami the fuck out of her. She hated it. But secretly loved it. We all did.

'Aye, Time Capsule,' I go.

We hold the moment for a bit, which softens all my body, and I know it does the same for him. He takes a very deep breath, his giant shoulders fall. His head is full of memories as well. I can tell.

'Anyway,' he goes, snapping out of the happy time. 'Do you want to come to this competition I'm in?'

I almost jump with shock at the surprise of his offer.

'Erm ...'

'You don't have to, it's just an idea. If you're busy, don't worry.'

'When is it?'

'Two weeks on Saturday.'

'Right,' I go, without showing any enthusiasm at all. I hate being this way with him. Life would be much easier if I could go *Aye, that's pure magic, cheers, Dad. Can I bring some of the troops with me.* But my face is searching for an excuse to say no. Any old excuse will do.

'Thing is, you'll need to let me know, so I can order tickets.'

'Freebies?'

Who doesn't like a freebie?

'Three.'

'So I can bring someone?'

He checks me out, top to toe. *Aye, you can bring two people, as long as it's none of those fuckwits you run around with . . . ?* Mum went to most of his comps; think she enjoyed being one of the muscle WAGs. Sometimes I can still hear their laughter when he'd come home with yet another trophy the size of a wean. Still see him tucking into normal dinners when a competition was over. Got to admire the cunt for the dedication he's put into it over the years. Just a pity he's not good at anything that pays top dollar, innit? We could be living in a four bedroom by now.

His shoulders rise up again; nods his head.

'Aye, you can bring someone,' he goes, then changes his stance, leans a wee bit closer to me. 'But don't make an arse of yourselves, all right? This isn't a fuckin' piss-take, Connor.'

'As if we would.'

He raises an eyebrow.

'So you want me to order them or not?'

Wee Z would love to go, he pushed me for tickets the last time Dad was competing. Naturally I knocked him back, telling him I'd have rather drunk pish out of shitey cloth. But given this is a freebie, he'll go bananas. Nails just thinks it's a Mickey Mouse posing challenge, a swinging dick contest. But, again, it's a freebie, so she'll be well into it. Trig, no chance . . . hundred per cent, that numpty would make an arse of himself. And everyone else.

'Aye, order me three then,' I tell him.

'Right.' He pats me on the arm. 'I'll get them sorted.' I nod my head in appreciation. 'There's chicken in the fridge, if you're hungry,' he goes as he's on his way out of the living room. 'I'm just gonna nip down to the gym, do an hour or so. You'll be OK here?'

'No bother.' Before he leaves we smile at each other. 'Dad?'

'Aye?'

'Cheers.'

Well, I think it's a smile.

When he's out the door I sprint up the stairs.

It's a toil. A graft. A headfuck. Leaves you worried for your self-esteem, something like this could knock you back to Fuck Town with your bawz stuck firmly between your legs. If you fail, you know you'll never attempt anything like this again in your puff. This isn't even your last chance, this is your only chance. Best to turn the lights out and forget about it forever. At least you tried, gave it a shot, mibbe even your best. Or did you? Did you just give up when it got a wee bit tough? A wee bit rough? Eh? Need a cuddle? Gave up, like everything else. School, for example, when you couldn't be fucked? Job searches, when you thought shovelling rubble was for stupid cunts like Trig or Wee Z? See, when stuff takes pain, thought and effort, that's when you quit, isn't it? That's you all over the back. You say, fuck it, and fire in the towel. So, please, do us all a favour and stop rabbiting on about escaping this place! With your attitude, you've got no chance. Let me tell you something, you thick bastard, you'll always remain here, ALWAYS, with that mindset. So get the finger out your arse and start again. And if it's shite, then start again. Make it more shite next time. And if that's still shite, then start again. And again. And again. Get the picture? That's the only way to get out of the treacle.

I breathe, take stock. Think deeply. Stare at the pages with the lines I've created. Loads scribbled out with black ink. Looks like Mr Messy spewed up all over it. I make a solid start on something that may or may not be about the future version of Trig. Might be about Sean. Nails's dad. Yobboy. Could be any crazy cunt at all.

I place my pen on the paper and let the wind and anger take me somewhere.

Crazy Cunt

I met this crazy cunt who told me how he betrays the law.
With conceited chest he bragged how he'd stab his da
                                    and batter his maw.
His frame festooned with
scars, scrapes, burns, bruises,
the resulting life that the hard-as-fuck guy chooses.

Crazy Cunt chewed my ear for an immeasurable
                                    period of time,
prattling about his new line in crime:
How doctors, teachers, policemen, nurses
were major players in this thing society curses.
Of how elected figures, vets and the Gogglebox brigade
are crucial in this murky parade.

BUT

See, when I learned that
students, D-list celebs, the greedy banker,
                                    the ballroom dancer,
(who all queued up for this cancer)
had been lambasted in some online rag
by some hypocritical hack
I was apoplectic with … indifference:

183

But I knew my role,

which was humouring this mad fucked-up blowhole:
I was like: *No way, mate you're having a laugh . . .*
Crazy Cunt frowned and said:
That's no even the half.

He then told me:
The private schoolies, buskers, wannabe comedians
and the *stand-up pro*
were all paying through their nose for his
                          substandard snow.

Then I did something slack:
questioned the prick's moral track.
Crazy Cunt glared,
eyes wide
nostrils flared . . .
none too chuffed.
He thought we were speaking the same language.
I surmised that he was seeking some
alpha-on-alpha praise.
Or acquiescence of his odious ways.
Cos all he was doing, he told me, was
meeting the demands of today's drug craze

and that I'd be *fuckin' surprised*
who's shovin it up their fuckin' hooter these fuckin' days.
Surprised?
No.

So after much toing and froing, Crazy Cunt
asked me if I wanted a wee gram for myself.
Naw, I'm all right mate, I telt him. *I don't believe*
that shite's too good for yer health.

He berated me,
sniggered at my prudence.
Crazy Cunt didn't take kindly to
common sense.
Subsequently the situation
got a wee bit tense.
Wit do you mean that shite's no good
for yer health?
When I explained the reason,
Crazy Cunt nodded and said:
I thought you were fuckin' tight, but I suppose yer
actually quite right.
Then he goes, after tightly gripping my hand:
But don't shoot me buddy,
cos I'm only the supply that meets the demand.

I sat alone when Crazy Cunt bolted.
Had five pints
Puffed seven fags
Inhaled a king-size doner
Pinballed home.
Sang some Rebel songs along the way.
A drunken cliché!

Woke up with a head like a burst couch.
Stomach a Bubonic sewer.
Throat a dog had shat in.

Sweat oozes.

The resulting life that a lawful-as-fuck man chooses:
Alcohol, Nicotine, Fast Food
all perfectly legit.
Not,
however,
to be sniffed it.

Post

Yobboy and his team have been at their pish again. Seems that Wee Z's got a part-time job trawling through Reddit and other shite sites that publish original Ned material. He came across another video post by those Fleeto bangers, fronted by the one and only. More ripping shreds out of us for doing fuck all about Biscuit; the whole gang bouncing about – head to toe in black – as if they were in some Brixton grime gang. Classic Hun activity. Laughable. Their desire for a proper ruck is dripping from them, right enough. Video was full of slashing motions, mimed machete swings and invisible handgun action. Total pish case, these wallopers couldn't even get their hands on a fuckin' spud gun. Saying that, you could smell the venom behind their gritted teeth.

Wee Z put it on the troops' group chat. No message. No words. Just a post left hanging for us to react to and some of us (Trig) to get riled over. When I first saw it my heart sank, not cos of the pish they were spouting or the threats against us or the slagging they were giving Biscuit again, but cos of the visions I had of Trig, livid as fuck. I see him rushing around his gaff, hooking holes in the gyprock walls. Crazy cunt, storming from room to room like a bull on heat. Then I see him making Millwall bricks as if he was in a Bangladesh sweatshop, steam billowing from his lugs. If anything I'd said to him got through, or was getting through to his senses, then it was going to be obliterated by that Fleeto video.

I was raging at Wee Z for posting; why not just keep it to yourself, you rocket? Trig'll be all over this like a bad rash now, hounding us; battering down our doors with a bag of paper weapons on his back. Ready to get up there and get fucked right into the lot of them, swinging blindly, scudding everything and anything that moves. Hard not to see casualties strewn over whatever battle street we'll be in; blood pishin' down drains. One-tens ruined with some cunt's blood. In the past I wouldn't have given two fucks about the consequences, but now when I picture the scene I'm one of those casualties. Eye socket gubbed. Teeth decked in. Jaw duffed up. Brain dented. A proper war scene that no one'll give a fuck about. And know why? Cos to them we're not human. Neds and human beings are very different things; like oil and water, they should never mix. We're a subspecies of a subspecies. Scheme urchins and nothing more.

I message Nails away from the chat.

See that?

Aye

                            Dicks. The lot of em

Aye

                            Trig'll be fuckin' bealin at it

Aye

                            Mentalist'll be wantin to chib sum Fleeto cunts

Aye

                            Don't let him get into yer head

No danger

                            Mean it, the guy's a loose canon

BOOM!!

*No joke Nails. Thinkin of
wee Z as well*

*Wee Z hasn't got the
bawz for aw that.
He'll be playin his
cricket*

Hope so

Me too

*Right, just thought I'd
mention it. Later*

No bother

So Nails was either not giving a flying fuck or her head was in a better place or she was cacking it, too. I'm not whining, just jealous; wish I'd that ability to flick a switch.

My stomach's bubbling with anxiety, it usually simmers at a safe and steady manageable level. See, I know what's coming and I know what's expected of me. And I know what the consequences will be if I bottle it: a friendship with Trig shattered, forever dodging the fists of him and his brother, being a known shitebag; living a different type of fight. But here's the God's honest, I've got no more fight in me. My desire to connect my fist or foot with a face just doesn't live in me any longer; even if I am spitting blood, which I'm not, and desperate to rattle some cunt, which I'm not, I don't feel it's part of me; that was a different Con. That guy died with his buddy Biscuit. And then there's the promise I made to Biscuit's mum. Can't forget that. Never will. *Loyal to the bitter end, wee man, eh.*

But, saying that, you know fine well that the anger, the desire to defend and do battle, will never truly leave you; always nipping away and scratching at your bones. Listen, let me tell you something, you might be desperate to escape, but you'll never escape from who you are, what you are and where you're from. Mean, you could be sitting in some bar in Timbukfuckintu, as far away from this town as possible, but you'll always be transported back. Something will crop up: a tiny wee nugget of insignificant nothingness. Nothing, yet something. Even the way you speak! You'll never be able to bolt from shite like that. No one can outrun their true identity, so I suggest you deal with it. Settle your differences with it and move the fuck on. OK, so you've said you're not into this any more, but deep inside you know that half of you wants to go up there alone and hunt out this Yobboy prick. Even if it's just to put it to bed. A last goodbye. Try and have a powwow with the guy. See if you both can stop this madness. When you clock him, you'll shout: *Deeno! Dean!*

Wee barra! Oi! Let's chat. You could find out what his address is, it would be a pure skoosh to get that info. You could fire that diss response through his letterbox. Peace at last.

But then again he did plunge your best mate to death, so mibbe a powwow is letting the wee dickhead off lightly; it isn't exactly the guilty verdict you're after. Who knows what to do. It's a toughy.

Or, alternatively, and this will take some serious thought on your part, you could pack a bag. Grab some dosh from somewhere, jump on a train and never look back. An anxious body sets the mind on fire. It starts crackling in all directions. It'll torture you if you remain.

I text Wee Z away from the chat.

> *Why u even sending that,*
> *ya spangle?*

Cos its nuts

> *Ur nuts for sending it on*
> *the group*

Fuck sake

> *Aye, fuck sake is right.*
> *Wait till Trig sees it*

*Wot did u want me to
do?*

> *Delete it. Forget about it.
> Say fuck all. That sort of
> thing*

And wot?

> *Wot u mean and wot?*

?

> *U prepared for the march
> up there eh? U got the
> skills required?*

It's not about that?

> *Wise up Z*

*Anyway that Fleeto mob
are asking for it*

> *Haha. Ur the one to give it
> to them r u?*

Didn't say I was, did I?

One question Z?

Wot?

*Are u going up there on
Sunday with Trig?*

Wee Z doesn't reply for ages. I see the three wee dots
blink and blink and then nothing. Guy's probably shaking
in his cricket pads. Wouldn't mind if Wee Z came from a
long list of mental fighting arseholes like Trig and Nails do,
but he doesn't. His mum and dad have decent jobs. I give
him thirty more seconds before hitting him with:

*Aye that's wot I thought.
But when Trig clocks that
video he'll be sharpening
his knuckles. U know that.
He'll be expecting handers.
So have a think about that*

I bet his brain is flashing as fast as those wee dots.

R u going, Con?

That's a fuckin' death
wish. Planned by Trig with
his last remaining brain
cell. U confident?

Always confident mate

Dont lie

Im no

There's always a way out

How?

DONT GO for a start

That wot ur thinkin?

Heads mangled Z not sure
wot am thinkin

They Fleeto twats need
there arses handed to
them tho

U believe that?

U dont?

No

*Eye for an eye and all
that*

*U go up there and ull have
no eyes left*

No chance

*I don't believe u don't want
to go Z. Deep down no*

The dots start to flash and stop again; well over five minutes. His thinking has gone into overdrive.

*Aye, but it's Trig we're
talkin about here Con.
How?*

*Just make yourself
unavailable*

Wot like run away?

*Or not meet him on
Sunday. There's a
difference Z*

Is there?

*Just think about Biscuit
and wot happened to him*

I am. I do

Me too

*And that makes me
want to smack some
cunt*

*Would you listen to yersel.
Wise up!!!*

*I better go, got cricket
practice later*

Yawn

After he sends a laughing emoji, I chuck my phone onto the bed and stick some NWA on. Crank up the volume. Drown out the other sounds floating around in my head. I fish out the bag Biscuit's mum gave me; rest it on my knees and stare at it. Sits there like a wee baby. I run a hand over it and scrunch it enough so it makes a rustling sound. NWA isn't doing it for me, full of death threats and gangsta shite. Still, it plays. I don't want to look inside again. I don't. But I know it's inevitable. I bring it up to my chest and let my face fall onto the bag. It stinks. That old mingin' plastic smell. My hands grip the two handle holes and I pull them apart. Honest to God, I don't want to look. I've never wanted to look. But that's exactly what I do. I look. And keep looking until the tears start to blur the two things that are inside.

CCTV

Hi Connor,

It's perfectly fine if you don't want to bring anything to read. Most people only bring themselves for the first few weeks. And don't worry about your lack of experience, you can simply observe, and when you are feeling confident enough, you can attempt something of your own. You don't even need to share with the rest of the group. Scottish Youth Poetry Group is about enjoyment and participation.

I wanted to share a poem that one of our new recruits did last week. This was only her second time attending, it's amazing what can be achieved in a week. Her name is Antonia, but she now goes by the name Toni D. (Mibbe you can think of a stage name, too.) The language is a bit fruity, but nothing you haven't heard before, I'm sure! I should warn you before you click that she does use words that could be deemed offensive – actually, some are highly offensive – which is the point, because that's what racism is.

Click the link and it'll take you to Toni D's poem, 'Your Racist Girlfriend'.

Hope to see you Sunday. We'll be in Studio 5, down the corridor to the left after you enter the building.

Vicky

Offensive words? Fruity language? That's right up my street. Link clicked. Toni D stands clutching onto the mic as if she's about to open her lungs and blast out some Goth tune. Black bob. Black lips. Black eyes. Fishnets ripped at the thighs. Mini skirt. Black. Pair of knackered Docs. Guess the colour. And a T-shirt with *St. Pauli* emblazoned across it. Never seen a girl wearing a German football team's T-shirt before. You just know she's gonna be like the rest of those poetry bangers: amazing.

> Couldn't believe that I wasted my time
> > yearning for *you*.
> Informing *you* of my favourite films and
> making up playlist after playlist
> full of hidden meanings:
> spewed my inner feelings.
>
> For a while I also listened to
> > Nine Inch Nails and The Cure

and stopped eating meat
but it didn't impress you that much.
So I had to admit defeat.

Yet whenever I saw you, my heart rattled like a
                                submachine gun.
If I'd been a proper Goth you'd have made
                                my make-up run.
I was crushed
confounded
infirmed
in-se-cure.
Which was something
The Cure couldn't even cure.

Cos of all the women you could have chosen,
why her and not someone else?

Excuse me for being blunt
but why did you hook up with
that horrible racist munt?

Don't you see it?
Don't you get it?
She doesn't love you, she's a different seed.
Don't you see it?

Don't you get it?
I could've given you all the love you need.
Don't you see it?
Don't you get it?
She's not like you or me:

She doesn't love the Neds, Taigs or junkies.
She doesn't love the skint, desperate or alkies.

She doesn't love the whores, scroungers or yobs.
She doesn't love the homeless, tinks or slobs.

She doesn't love the beige, browns or blacks.
She doesn't love the Jews, Paddies or Polaks.

She doesn't love the gays, trans or queer breed.
She doesn't love folk from a different creed.

She doesn't love PEOPLE, EVE!
And, really,
is there any other love you need?

Yet another slammer to put you right in your place. This time it doesn't make you feel like a useless fake though, you actually feel inspired. So much so, you go onto listen to Toni D again, before trawling back through Ginger Archie's, PaulaTik's and the two other lads' stuff once more. There's no chance you'd ever be as good as them, that's a given. You don't pretend otherwise. But mibbe, just mibbe, your experience is equal to theirs. Your life is as valid as theirs, that's for sure. Don't forget that. Doesn't matter what poems you produce or how you deliver them; sometimes words aren't the important thing: it's feelings and emotions that drive a person. Like everyone else on this earth, you breathe and think and talk and feel. So you exist like those poetry folk, too. If you don't go to that fuckin' thing on Sunday you're basically shutting yourself down; you'll always remain voiceless. And if you let anyone steal your voice, you'll be nothing more than a bystander in life, you'll have no control over anything, no original thought. You're the only one who knows what you require, so take it by the throat and discover your voice. But my question is this: why wait for others to say what you're feeling? Why not say it yourself? I know you want to escape the scheme, but the first steps come from within, you don't need to be physically somewhere else in order to be free, you know. Go on, you can do it, you can do anything. Fine, you could read that 'Crazy Cunt' poem, it's not too bad, but do you really want to be that guy who's brimming with that amount of anger? You want to impress, not shock them. Remember, you're more than an angry Ned, Connor O'Neill. Much more.

There's a warmth in my body. OK, listening to De La Soul's *3 Feet High and Rising* will do that. One of Mum's favs back in the day, so she told me. She used to sing some of it to me when I was a wean; I'll take her word for it. The warmth comes from the fact that Vicky Rooney went out her way to contact me, she didn't need to do that. She doesn't know me from Adam. Mibbe if she did, she'd tell me to sling it and not to come anywhere near her poetry group. But she didn't. She spat out her reassurance and showed me what can be achieved. How can I not go now? Apart from pressure from Trig, the lust for revenge and the opportunity to smash some skulls, what's stopping me? Want. Desire. Fear.

Hi Vicky,
Thanks for the email. I really appreciate you sending the Toni D poem. Like all the others it was pretty spectacular. I don't think I'm at that stage yet, but I can just watch, as you say.
Mibbe see you Sunday.

Connor

As soon as I press send I hear *SLAM!* Geezer nearly fucks the front door off its hinges. The whack reaches me in my room. Louder than De La Soul. For a split I think we're getting robbed, then I calm down, knowing that there's fuck all to rob. From the top of the stairs I hear him groaning in the living room.

Thank fuck it's only Dad, I think. Also, fuckin' hell, it's Dad! It's impossible to tiptoe down our stairs without masking the sound of creaky steps. That's me nabbed, got to go to him now, haven't I? Show concern.

Deep breath.

He's sat forward on the chair, hand clutching his forehead as if he's in deep thought. Pain's spanked all over his coupon. He doesn't flinch in my presence. Doesn't even acknowledge that I'm standing in front of him.

'Dad.' He looks at me through the open slits of his fingers. 'What happened?'

'Go get me some ice.'

Ice!

We don't have any. The wee plastic tray that makes that shite ice is empty. All we have is a bag of a decade-old frozen sweetcorn. That'll do. Have to. I hand it to him and he presses it against his swollen forehead. Holds it tight and grimaces. Either he's been putting the nut on walls or some cunt's banjaxed him. There's a tiny cut on the bridge of his nose, more of a scrape, really. If he'd been in his bouncer gear I'd have put two and two together by now, understood that he'd been set upon by a couple of steamers, but he's in his gym clobber. Bag chucked on the couch. I'm not sure he actually made it to the gym; doesn't look like a man who's done a workout. He cracks his neck left to right and back again. I move closer for a better swatch.

'Don't worry, Connor, it looks worse than it is,' he goes.

I was actually thinking that it doesn't look that bad; wee bit of swelling on the napper, few red marks. I go closer. God, the way he's leaning on that sweetcorn, you'd think he'd been poleaxed by a bus; I've had worse doings, and that's when I've come out on top.

'You might have a bruise the morra,' I go. 'But nothing more than that, I'd say.' I sound like the resident expert in all things facial injury.

'Aye. I'll be fine.'

'What happened?'

He presses the sweetcorn harder against his face. His chest heaves; he looks up at me for the first time. Bloodshot eyes; puffed-up to fuck. Must've been some scud. I recognise my eyes in his, or his in mine. Some people used to say we were the spit of each other, I've never seen it cos I can't see past the muscles. Here I do, though. Sad eyes. Some said it was Mum I was the spit of. You wouldn't know who to believe? Different day, different spit.

'Dad, what's the score here?'

He juggles the sweetcorn between his hands, making them wet. Wipes his sodden face. Can't make out if the moisture is from angry tears or from the defrosting veg.

'Fuckin' arseholes jumped me,' he goes.

'What arseholes?'

'Two of them, acting the big men.'

'Who?'

'Think they were after the bag.'

'What? That thing?' I nod to his gym bag on the couch.

'Aye.'

'So they slapped you around in order to get that bag?'

'Arseholes,' he says, and returns the sweetcorn to his dome.

'For a bit of gym gear?'

'Aye.'

'Right.'

I knew he was talking pish. Mean, who wants to rob some stinking gym bag? And who in their right mind wants to rob from a man mountain who could knock you out in a matter of seconds? Makes fuck all sense.

'Where did it happen?'

'Just before I got to the gym.'

'Aye, but where exactly?'

He looks at me as if I'm accusing him of something suspicious. His eyes change. Definitely *not* the spit of me.

'At the industrial estate where the gym is. Capiche?' he says slowly, in a voice you'd rattle off to the polis when the pricks start fuckin' with you.

'That's good then,' I go.

'How?'

'Cos one of the businesses in that industrial estate will have CCTV. You'll be able to have a gander.'

'Aye, well, we'll see about that.'

'Did they hit you with something?' I bob and weave to get a better view of his second prize. 'Cos it looks as if they might've, you know.'

'Aye, they might've. Something fuckin' hit me, that's for sure.' He hands me the bag of frozen sweetcorn, which is fully dripping through both our hands. 'All happened too fast.'

'But you knew there were two of them though?'

'Aye, for fuck sake!' he spits.

'Well, you should have a gander at thon CCTV then, you'll definitely find out who tried to pan your lights in.'

His puffy eyes are in no mood for this chat. They might fire similar daggers to Denise's, but they can't hide the bullshit that's behind them.

'You better put that back in the freezer –' he nods to the frozen sweetcorn – 'before it gets all over the carpet.'

'Think there's carrots in there, want some carrots?'

'No, I'll be fine.'

'Right,' I go, trying to show concern. Worry. Whatever. Basically trying not to grill him any more about the shite he's spouting; hard to stop myself from calling him a big dirty lying bastard. Tell you one thing, if this *attack* happened for real he'd be all over that CCTV footage in a heartbeat, ready to rip the head off some cunt. I know him like the back of my hand.

'I'm OK, honestly,' he grimaces. 'You don't need to worry about me.'

'Someone's got to.' I grin at him and head for the freezer.

'Connor,' he calls after me.

'Aye?'

'You should get out of here.'

I lift the bag of sweetcorn up towards my face and try to catch some of the dripping water.

'I might nip down to Nails's—'

'Not this house,' he goes. 'This place. This town.'

'Aw, right.'

I'm not floored by the fact that he didn't say *we*. I'm not floored at all, just surprised. Could be the concussion. Why else would his thinking be skewed? Water falls from the bag and hits my one-tens.

'You really should get out of this town.' His face is soft and serious. He means it. Does he want to get rid of me? His only child. Is that it? What parent tells their kid to bolt? 'I'm serious, Connor.'

'Well, that could be a plan,' I go.

'This place has got fuck all goin' for it.'

Is that right? *Fuck all goin' for it?* Tell me something new. Think I don't know a place like this will destroy your life? Will chew you and keep chewing until the bitter end? That's true. But only if you let it.

If. You. Let. It.

Think I won't be telling posh cunts, snobs or people who live by the coast how much I love this place? Course I will. Think I don't know deep down that it'll never love me back? Course I do. But only if I let it.

If. I. Let. It.

'It's not that bad,' I go, wondering why I'm trying harder to stick up for the shithole.

'Not that bad?' he goes. 'It's nothing but a big mental health ward.' I nod. He's not wrong. He's not right either. 'If you want to find happiness in your life then you need to get out.' It takes a lot for me not to fire his own statement right back at him. Or pish myself laughing. If there's anyone in my network who's in dire need of some happiness, it's this geezer.

Is it happiness you're after? Aye, no bother, I'll just get myself shifted before I make the big move. I'll start by popping this sweetcorn back in the freezer then fold some T-shirts. Get the toiletries sorted. Empty the bank account of its twelve quid and buy a one-way ticket to Fantasyville. The 100k-a-year job kicks in on Monday. Can you give me a lift to the station when your swelling goes down? I'll give you a buzz when I get there.

Seriously, you've got to laugh at times; these people are rubbish role models for this generation fuck-up. People like my dad who've spent a lifetime suffering, always spout the same old shite: you've got to leave to survive. That's their one and only solution: get the fuck out of Dodge. No trying to fix it from within or thinking better, smarter and more imaginatively. No, it's always down to, go and don't return. Fine, we'll all get the fuck out, book a giant bus. But tell us how; give us the means to do it. Where do we even go? A big city that'll strip us of our identity and home comforts? Or do we just rock from one shite town to the next until we're put in a box? Show us how to make that first step? It's guidance we're after, not dosh. Well, there is that.

Right enough, the biggest motivation of them all is seeing the future reflected right back at you, in this case my old man sitting there as if life's devoured him, gave him some ridiculous-looking muscles, and spewed him back out again. Who in their mad mind let this clown become a father?

'Mibbe I'll find happiness here,' I go. 'Get a decent job, a wee flat.'

'Heard anything from the Time Capsule yet?'

'Not yet.'

Truth is I didn't even check their website to see. Typical me. Typical me. Typical me. I'll do it tonight; quick fill-out of some online form. Doddle. Job'll practically be mine.

He shakes his head. Aaannnddd, we're back to disappointed Dad.

'Don't end up like your . . .' He slouches back into the chair without saying the word Mum or mother or Biscuit or old man.

Hate that sound the freezer makes when something's being squeezed into it. The noise of ice scratching and falling off the sides doesn't half pierce my skull. That's the sound of our gaff, my life, every movement I make; every thought I have seems to scratch the fuck out of my skull. I'm the one who's in dire need of defrosting.

Dad shouts at me from the hall.

'I'm going up for a lie down, Connor.'

'No bother.'

'Head's rocking.'

'Aye, bed's probably the best place for you.'

'Aye.'

'Can I get you anything?'

'No, just keep the noise down.'

'No bother.'

'Right, then.'

'Right.'

Before he ambles up the stairs, we have a mini stare-off for a few seconds. He knows I know something; knows I'm not as daft as I look. I'll find out what the craic is. Mark my words. Cunt can't kid a kidder.

Landfill

This is the second time I've been here. Always meant to come again on a solo mission, but, you know, what's the point? All this public outpouring of grief feels a bit self-harmy, if you ask me. I don't think any of the others have been back either; if they have, they've kept it to themselves. How's that for honour among thieves?

There's no joy for me being back in this spot; isn't the place where my memories are flooded with magic days of happiness. Nothing was calling me back. Promised never to return, had to practically drag myself here, kicking and screaming, but there you go. OK, so this is the place where we sank the odd half-bottle, listened to tunes and smoked joints galore, but not much else. Well, that and ran a few battles with whatever squad wanted it. All our banter and bliss happened in school or in our gaffs, not here in this excuse for a park.

The only evidence that something significant happened here is a deflated balloon that's been stubbed into the wet grass. Number eight still visible. That's the only thing that remains, unless you include the fact that the grass is patchy from the shower of nosy bastards' feet. Seems like yesterday the four of us were sifting through all the shite people had left at the scene; a monument of grief created in front of our very eyes. Seeing that for the first time hit me hard. I know it hit all of us hard, but we did that thing we do in the schemes of trying to hide our sadness; scared of showing our pain for fear of someone ripping the pish out of you. We sashayed round the shrine, and each other, without having anything substantial to do or say; so we reverted to type and ridiculed the people who'd left stuff behind. And then there was Trig, strutting about, spitting blood, laying down the law of the land with his low-level threats and taunts. That's the memory I've got as I stand here freezing my tits off.

I stroke my neck, trying to feel for the lump that was lodged in my throat that day, seeing if I can somehow recreate it. I swallow. It's gone. It's all gone.

Still, I want that day back. I do.

I want to read all the cards and messages without slagging the fuck out of them. I want to straighten out all the Celtic tops, see him running away, arms aloft, as if he's just scored a last minute winner against the Huns. I want to roll the communion candles down my face and remember the pair of us in our spanking school uniforms on that sunny Saturday, hands rigid in the praying position. Delighted with all the money we'd be getting later; our spending plans. But nothing remains. Biscuit's life taken twice now. First by the Fleeto, then by the council. You think any of the council guys gave consideration to his life when they were fuckin' all the stuff into landfill? Some mother's wean. Some guy's best mate. Poor Biscuit.

Stubbing my foot into this empty patch, my mind's running wild with itself. I'm thinking, who drank the two half-bottles of Buckie? Who's got that picture with Biscuit on Mrs McVitie's knee? Did everything get chucked? Then I'm wondering if Trig and his brother blagged those Celtic tops and tried to punt them. Wouldn't put it past the cunts. Can totally see them sinking the Buckie, too.

To me, this stubbed balloon is much more depressing than that grotesque shrine ever was; hurts me harder than a sledgehammer would. Imagine being reduced to nothing more than a deflated balloon, a deformed bit of rubber. Thing is, when the grass eventually grows back people will forget anything happened here. It'll be known as that patch where some Ned got murdered; some wee lowlife got their comeuppance. Even that memory will quickly float away to nowhere fast. And then what? Just another patch of grass in a park that's not fit for purpose; no football, no swings, no fun. The thought of having a picnic here is a pish case anyway. The council have got some cheek to call this abomination an amenity, some numpties need their bawz handed to them for inflicting our community with this; a place where you'd think twice about letting your dog shite in. But, that's it, isn't it? That's all we're good for: wet grass, broken glass and dog shite. This place doesn't belong to me or the troops any longer, the glory days are over; time for a different set of disaffected fuckwits to get puggled on Buckie and bleamed on some brother's super skunk. But, hundred per cent, you can count on another shrine popping up in a different part of this park soon enough. In umpteen years to come, the place will be dotted with shrines of all the stabbed and speared of this town. And, other than family members and mates, not a cunt will care.

You do a full three-sixty twirl on your heels, your stupid way of getting a final look at the place. For whatever reason only you know, you drop to your knees, lean onto all fours and then rest your face on the dewy grass, arse sticking up in the air. There's a picture of you somewhere sleeping like this when you were a wean. You're lying like this cos you know wild horses won't be able to drag you back in the future. Ever. So there's a need for you to feel him rushing through your veins one last time, to apologise for not protecting him that night; for not trying to get you both away from this shite sooner. He needs to know that you're desperately gonna fight for the dreams you both made together. This is why you're lying here in the snoozing baby position, cos you feel a strong need to tell him. You have to let him know how you feel zero guilt for wishing it would've been Trig instead, you don't want to blab on about that, but you can't help yourself.

Don't bother yersel with that shite, Con.

It's true, it should've been him, though.

Should've been, could've been.

If anyone relished the battle more than any of us, it was that headcase.

Save yer energy, mate. Let it go.

Cunt was always a shoo-in to get the first shrine among us. It's no fair, wee man.

It could've been any one of us; could've been you, you know.

Fuck that!

Aye, tell me about. Fuck that, is right.

I'd have brought Trig a 'Told you so' flag and planted it bang in the middle of his shrine.

Nick of us, back then though!

Nick of me now.

Aye, stop snogging the grass and get up, ya stupid cunt.

Love ye, wee man.

Aye, you too. Now, get the fuck up before you gee us both a red neck.

Keep yer bunnet on.

The wind whistles through my ears and hair, my eyes are closed so that tears don't drip onto the grass. Are these tears from sadness or Baltic winds? Fuck if I know. Sometimes it's hard to tell who's suffering from cold or weather in this town. Everything's dark, my mind takes me back to the five of us together in this park. Not one particular moment in time, more like six years squeezed into a blaring mishmash of doomed youth. The five of us, cutting about idle; the fizz of voices play loud in my head. We're all barking over one another, as usual, each of us trying to be top dog, crack the best joke, dole out the biggest put-down, slag the hardest. If I'm being truthful, Biscuit was the one who mostly came out on top. He was by far the smartest. Our voices then drift away as quickly as they came, the wind and the zip of the passing cars is all that's left. Then everything suddenly goes dead, no sound at all.

And the air changes.

I feel a presence behind me; she's returned again, this time kneeling and stroking my sunken head. Her nails sharp against my neck. I don't take myself out of this position but I know exactly how she's looking, I can smell her red lipstick and those Maxwell House eyes. I inhale her fragrance into my bones. Feel like I'm floating on air. When she speaks her voice tickles my ear:

Hiya, son.

Hiya, Mum.

You used to sleep in this position when you were a baby.

So I'm told.

I wish I could go back to those days.

Do you?

I'd change it all if I could.

Change what?

Everything.

Think I'm beginning to know what that emotion feels like now.

I know you do, son, and that's why I'm here.

Why are you here?

To tell you something.

What?

Not to ruin your life wishing you could go back somewhere; not to have a life brimming with regrets, not to have sleepless nights because you're longing for something you almost got your hands on.

Do you regret leaving us? Leaving me? Is that a regret?

Every day, Connor. There's not a day that goes by when I don't. You know I'd never do anything to hurt you.

Well, you did. You have. I still hurt. I hurt all the time. Now, thanks to you, I'm that guy whose mum, you know . . .

And I can't take that back. No words can ever soothe your pain, I understand that. That's the regret I'm talking about. I'll be forever sorry.

It's OK, I know you are. It's just . . .

You know what you have to do, Connor, don't you?

I think so, yes.

OK, I'll leave you to consider it.

Thanks.

I love you.

Me too.

My nose still searches for her fading fresh smell. When it fully disappears, I'm disappointed. All that remains for me is the dirt and wind. My breathing is shallow, but my chest is light as a feather for the first time in ages. The floating sensation is still in me. The best stone ever. I start counting in my head, promising to bounce up as soon as I hit number ten. I count slowly. It's somewhere in the count, around the five or six, when things become clear: I know what I have to do. I might not know exactly how to do it, but I know something has to be done, and it doesn't require any violence. Fuck that.

She's bang on.

TEN.

I snap to my feet and blow hot air through my hands.

Some old dear walks past, tugging a French bulldog. When she glances in my direction my head automatically drops and I start digging my heel on Biscuit's deflated balloon, burying it deeper into the soggy grass. The one-tens get battered in the process. The old dear knows fine well what used to be here, course she does, it's part of her route. Bet she had a good old snoop when the shrine was in full swing. A colour fest; an exhibition for all-comers to gawk at. No ticket required. I don't look up at her, but I can tell her face is a picture of hate. No doubt she saw me lying here and thought I was just another junkie/alkie fucked out his nut, an addition to the human litter clogging up her town. Somebody should tell her to write a heated letter to her MP – for all the good that'll do – to see if she can get us chucked into landfill as well. Ask anyone who our MP is and they'll most likely tell you that they haven't a fuckin' scooby. A twat who's never lived here, that's who. Actually, I don't blame the old dear, some scruffy cunt cutting about alone in a park isn't someone you're drawn to, is it? I watch her drag the Frenchie in the opposite direction, there's a fear and urgency in her walk; seen so many people make that exact walk a thousand times before. Not her fault, but the old dear makes me feel ashamed to be here, and mibbe I am. Ashamed to be me. Shame is a weird beast, always sniffing and lurking about. These days it never leaves me alone. I wipe my face, shove my hands inside my Puma hoodie and head towards Nails's gaff. She doesn't know I'm about to drop in on her, but she soon will. Some words of warning are best served face to face. You need to be able to see the look in the eyes, the way the jaw opens; the face's honesty.

Ambulance

After Wee Z, Nails's got the best gaff. They moved into her gran's old place after she died. Shares a garden with an old couple who never use it. Result! Mean, it's not a garden full of flowers or plants, it's basically a bit of grass with four clothes poles that square it off. *Garden* elevates it, to be fair; everyone just calls it 'out the back'. Her mum's washing is always hung up; every time you're out the back, something's flapping around your napper. Since she lost her job at Nail Diamonds, that's all that poor woman does. Nails's mum manicured nails in Nail Diamonds, ever since I can remember and then, one day, BANG! Out on her ear. Just like that, no warning, no explanation. No rights. Fuckin' criminal, man. I might be wrong, but I think she met Nails's old man in the pub next door, he used to work behind the bar. Aye, cos that's what you do if you're an alkie, you search for jobs with easy access to booze. Just like you'll find loads of sex pests working in schools. Nails regularly hides behind the fluttering sheets to practise some of her moves. It's a sight and a half. Can't really blame the old couple for staying indoors, can you?

After visiting Biscuit's shrine I'm feeling a bit like the sky and buildings: miserable as fuck. I'm hoping Nails'll be able to put a grin back onto my coupon. Cup of tea at least, cos the wind would slice the face off you. An ambulance rockets past me, blue light flashing and siren blazing. Fuck sake, I mutter, is it necessary to have that thing blaring as loud? It's hardly trying to get itself through a traffic jam in rush hour, is it?

Nails's street is like one of those towns in a Western film: dead and sinister. You feel eyes on you every step you take. It's also a mess; an assault course of weans' bikes, scooters and wheelie bins. You wouldn't dare think about having a go on any of the bikes as the street polices itself. You'd get your hand cut off if you even thought about blagging one. The bins have all been emptied, people just can't be arsed to take them in; daytime TV is too good to be dragged away from. A few curtains twitch, which is normal. I'm fine, my face is known. Been coming here for years. I'm safe, for now. It's the next generation of maddies you need to worry about, those who don't know your face from back in the day, so you become a target. On a sunny day Nails's street is like a poor man's version of Alton Towers.

I stick the brakes on when I see her and do a kinda double-take. Nails's sitting on the step, smoking a fag. Plume clouds wafting above her head. Puffing that shite into her lungs won't bring Olympic glory, that's for sure. She's always loathed smoking, so what holy fuckery is this? Automatically I know something's not right with the scene.

'Nails!' I shout as I walk up her path. She looks at me and flicks the lit fag high into the air soon as our eyes lock. 'What the fuck you all about?' I point to the discarded fag.

'Don't start, Con.' Her voice is a mixture of fear and aggression. There's a shudder to it.

When I get to the steps she's sitting on, I clock the pack of Marlboro Gold; her hands are shaking, fingers twitching. Her knees bob up and down as well. Nothing to do with the cold.

'You OK, Nails?' I go, trying to soften my voice and sound sympathetic. 'Something happen?' She's tears in her eyes; face burning with whatever fury she's carrying. 'Who gave you the fags?' Her jaw is tight and quivers slightly.

'They're his,' she manages to get out.

'Whose?'

'Excuse of a fuckin' dad of mine.'

'What, he gave you them?'

'I took them.'

She pulls another from the pack and sticks it in her mouth. Nails isn't a smoker – the weird way it sags from her lips would tell you that – so everything about this feels so fucked-up and scary. And another thing, you don't rock up and blag your dad's fags either. Especially not hers. Clearly she's zero desire to hear me wag on about how taekwondo and fags are a match made in Hell. A bit like us and the Fleeto.

'I was just down visiting Biscuit's wee shrine there,' I go, hoping to snap her out of it. She doesn't even flinch or feign interest. 'Or what's left of it.' Her eyes wander off into the distance.

'I don't want to think of Biscuit, Con. My head's fuckin' rammed with thinking about all that shite. Just want it to go away and not touch me again.'

'Yeah, I know. I'm with you.'

She yanks the unlit fag from her mouth and crushes it in her hand, the loose tobacco falls at her feet. That's when I notice the spots of red on the toe of her one-tens.

'Fuck's that on your trainer?' I ask. 'Is that blood?'

She examines the trainer before taking a wet thumb to it. Could've told her it would've smudged.

'Aye, must be,' she goes.

'Whose?'

'His.'

'His who?'

'The old man's.'

I flick my neck back in shock and instantly regret doing it. But what other reaction is there? My foot comes off the bottom step; I stand up straight and steady myself for the onslaught of something massive.

'Nails? What the fuck happened?'

She slaps the rest of the tobacco away from her hands, it falls like breadcrumbs over her, then she grogs a few belters onto her palms. With the spit she tries with more oomph and better technique to scrub the blood off the one-tens. I decide to say nothing of the bawz up she's making. The toe of her trainer looks pink. The more she rubs, the worse it gets, the worse it gets, her fury rises.

'Fuck it!' she blasts and stops her Mr Sheen routine. Wipes her palms on her trackie bottoms. Cracking New Balance pair, as well.

'Mix some lemon juice and bicarbonate soda together,' I tell her, one of Mum's many tricks. 'And that'll be like new in no time.' If there's one thing I've experience of, it's getting blood out of trainers. Now I need to get it out of a stone. I want to grip her knee and reassure her. Of what, I don't know yet, but I need to at least let her know I'm here.

'Nails.' She looks up. 'Talk to me, buddy. What's going on?'

She wipes her face and sighs.

'I was coming back from the gym,' she starts. 'And I heard them from the street.'

'Heard who?'

'Mum and Dad, well, Dad mainly, screaming the whole fuckin' place down.'

'From inside the house?'

'Aye.'

'Oh, right. Shit. That's not good, is it?'

'Going at it like fuck. He was giving it full pelt.'

I want to ask if her dad was pished, but, of course he was pished, he's always pished. That's what alkies do, isn't it? Time of the day is not an issue for them. I look up at her gaff expecting to hear some noise from inside, but it's like a monastery. In fact, there's an eerie silence from the whole street. Just hoping her mum put enough milk in his tea or beans on his toast. That's the fear the poor woman lives in.

'Where is your—?'

'Not a sinner helped.' She nods to the surrounding houses. 'They all fuckin' heard it, but not one of them did a thing.'

Not a surprise. You don't get caught up in anyone's disputes around here, especially a domestic. That's a sure way to get your windows panned or your head kicked in, or both. It's a danger to be a Good Samaritan in this town, they're seen as interfering bastards and nothing else. Nails knows this.

'Mibbe they just didn't want to get involved,' I go, stating the bloody obvious.

'Not one of them lifted a fuckin' finger, Con. Not even phoned the polis.'

Again, she knows that this is a red line round here. It's just her emotion yapping.

'Where is your mum now?' I finally ask. 'Is she in the

house? Is she OK?' She stares at the pink-coloured toe of her one-tens and something chimes in me. A thought scuds me, makes me wobble. 'Nails, where's your dad?'

She hits me with these eyes, a look that could burn paint off a door.

'He's a cunt, and deserves all he got,' she goes.

My heart starts racing, adrenalin rushes through my bloodstream. My brain automatically thinks the worst. Her eyes don't let me believe that there's anything else to think. All of a sudden she seems as if she's not in her own thoughts. That's when I grip onto her knee.

'Nails!' I say firmly. 'What the fuck happened here?' I squeeze her knee hard to show that I'm not messing around. My mind's running away with itself. Blood. Her fear. Her fury. Her trainers. Now I'm thinking the worst, that he's lying in there with a steak knife sticking out his temple, gargling on his own vomit, a crimson halo of blood surrounding his dome.

'Is your dad in the house?'

She shakes her head. Tightens her lips. Sucks air in through her nose.

'I put my dad in an ambulance, Con. That's what happened.'

My ambulance? That one that flew past me minutes ago? That one with its blue light roaring? That sound-polluting fucker? *That* ambulance?

'Is he OK?' I go. 'I mean, what did you do that he ended up in an ambulance?'

'He was booting fuck out of her. When I ran in, she was on her knees and he had her by the hair, she was helpless, couldn't do anything. Cunt was pure rag-dolling her, Con. Kept punching the fuck out her face and head. She'd blood all over her. Screaming at him to stop.'

'Fuckin' hell, Nails, mate.'

'I tried to boot him on the head but luckily for him I only caught his chest. Then he bolted, or tried to. I chased him outside.'

'I'm taking it you caught him then?'

'Bastard was too pished to get anywhere, he was mid-fall when I caught up with him.'

'And?'

'And I wellied the cunt two belters in the face. The second boot made his head crack against the wall and split open. When he fell forwards, it was like slow motion. He was out cold. Everything rolled out his pockets. Fags. Lighter. Coins. I thought I'd killed him, Con. No joke.'

'Who phoned the ambulance?'

'Mum.'

'Your mum!'

'She was roaring at me to stop.' Nails lets out a wee snigger. 'How fuckin' mental is that? She's running out, nose splattered all over her coupon, telling me to stop knocking fuck out the guy who'd just knocked fuck out of her.' Her snigger turns into a growling bark. 'How can you keep loving someone like that?'

'I don't know. It's beyond me.'

'Pair of them deserve each other.'

'They just need help,' I go, not knowing what else to say.

Nails leans forward and her eyes widen. She screams: '*I* need fuckin' help, Con. Me!'

'Aye, I know, mate. I know. I'm sorry.'

She stands up and wipes flakes of tobacco off her New Balance trackie. Launches the pack of Marlboro Gold into a neighbour's garden. Swears at them under her breath.

'She went in the ambulance with him, you know.'

'Who?'

'Mum.'

'Oh, right.'

'A two-for-one job.'

'Was your dad OK? Mean, were they both OK?'

'He came round, they stuck a collar on him. A few stitches. Seven, ten at most. Prick'll be in the pub for last orders.'

'Aye, probably.'

'They packed Mum's nose, that was it.' Nails starts skelping the palm of her hand with a closed fist, not aggressively, more thoughtfully. 'She'll have to answer for it though, won't she?'

'You don't know that, mibbe this'll be a turning point.'

'If it happens again, I swear I'll kill the cunt. I told him that as they were lifting him into the ambulance.'

'Did he say anything?'

'Dick didn't know if it was New York or New Year, but I'm telling you, one more time and he's fucked. I'm deadly serious, Con.'

'I know, mate. I know.'

'Anyway, fuck him. My head's mangled thinking about him all the time.'

I want to ask if we can go inside, as it's brass monkeys. But don't really want to see the scene of the crime right enough. I'll battle on regardless.

'Know what I think, Nails?' I go.

'What?'

'We just need to get out of this fuckin' place.'

'No shit.' She stops punching her palm. Her expression makes me feel stupid for stating the bleedin' obvious. 'You think all this training I do, the effort I put in, the sacrifices, are for fuck all, do you?'

'No, anything but.'

'I've no interest in medals and trophies, Con. My plan is to get the fuck out of here as quickly as possible; to get me some lottery funding, sponsorship, whatever, and bolt from this fuckin' shithole. Never look back. Never come back.'

'No, I get that. Totally know what you mean.'

'And see all that shite with Trig and his paper brick or whatever the fuck it's called?'

'Aye?'

'Well, he can ram that right up his arse as well. I've had it with fighting other people's battles.' She starts with the palm punching again. 'We can't bring Biscuit back.'

'I know that.'

'Nothing we do will fix anything. In fact, it'll only make things worse. The best thing for us to do is bury it, leave all our anger or sadness or whatever the fuck you want to call it in the ground with Biscuit.'

'I'm with you on that.'

The punches morph into a hand rub; think the cold is setting in.

'And now it's time to get my release paper from this town,' she goes.

'Mine too,' I go, slightly excited that she's said this. 'I want the exact same thing as you.'

Nails twists her neck as though I'm talking out my hole. As though I don't deserve the same opportunities as her. As though having a talent for a martial art is the only thing that can ever set you free from here.

'You can't go, Con,' she goes. 'You can't leave here.' The sympathy in her voice almost knocks me over. 'How can you?'

'How can I not?'

She does her weird neck thing again.

'Well, cos of your dad.'

Now it's my turn to twist my neck towards her, give her the old what-the-fuck-you-talking-about look.

'What the fuck are you talking about, Nails?'

'Who's gonna look after him?'

'He can look after himself, he's a big boy.'

'Come on, Con, you know what I mean.'

Ah, then it dawns on me. I get it. The elephant in the room finally makes an appearance.

'You on about my mum?' I go.

'Aye, a bit, but not just that.' She takes a breath, as if she's setting herself up to another revelation. 'Look, I know your dad is sometimes a champion cunt these days.'

'Whose isn't?'

'Exactly. But before . . . you know . . . your mum and all that, you two used to get on awright.'

'Used to.'

'I was a wee bit jealous when I saw you havin' the craic together. I know Trig was.'

I scrunch up my face.

'Of me and my dad?'

'Aye. Were you not good mates at one point?'

I clench my fist and start punching it softly against my thigh. Swimming. Cinema. Football. Parks. TV. Tunes. We did it all back in the day. Mean, it's not a conscious thing, but I feel my head nodding in agreement with Nails.

'At one point.'

'Con, the shit that's happened. You and your dad . . . you fuckin' need each other.'

'Look, what happened to Mum, happened. It's not my fault, or Dad's. She fucked up, which isn't a crime, by the way. And I'm not saying what she did didn't fuck us up, too, but what are you expecting me to do? Hide in my room for the rest of my life? Spend all my days here, in this fuckin' kip, with the memory of my mum's actions battering off my skull? You want me and Dad to just go on suffering?' She shakes her head. 'Thought so. See, I want more, too, Nails. I need more.'

'Who doesn't?'

'The old man's the one who told me to get away from here, in any case.'

'Good, hope to fuck you take heed.'

'Do I ever?'

Nails raises an eyebrow.

'Mr Sensible, me.'

'So, what's the plan then, Con?'

'Same as yours, get some money behind me then blow town.'

'Sounds solid to me.' I'm unsure if she's being sarcastic or not. My instincts tell me she is. I haven't said anything about the Time Capsule job, you never know, I might get it. 'Know what else I'm planning?' I go.

'What?'

'To be somewhere else this Sunday. Head into Glasgow or something.'

Nails's face contorts with the realisation of what Sunday means.

'Aye, Sunday,' she goes.

'You're not going, are you?'

'You having a laugh? Am I fuck.'

'Good to know,' I chuckle, and put out my fist for a bump. 'Not much of an organiser, is our Trig.' We hit knuckles. 'Worst idea he's had. Wee Z's up for it though.'

'What?'

'Aye, I know.' I throw up my arms like a pissed-off teacher. 'He's wanting to hand someone their arse. I tried to tell him—'

'Wee Z?'

I nod.

'That's fuckin' insanity,' Nails spits, shakes her head disbelievingly. 'You summed it up at his place, it's a death wish.'

'Even with Wee Z, he'll be looking for handers. For you.'

'Aye, well, he'll be looking forever, won't he?'

'You know what he's like.'

'If he starts any of his pish, he'll get what Dad got.'

'Why not come with me on Sunday?' I go. Don't know why I say this. Heat of the moment stuff. Brain not engaged with mouth. Mibbe I'm feeling sorry for Nails cos she knocked fuck out of her dad. Big softy, me. This was to be my thing and my thing alone. A secret. My own personal mafia. But could be good to have a sidekick. Safety in numbers and all that. Not that I'm scared . . . OK, a bit.

'Where you off to?' Nails goes.

'Just somewhere near Queen Street Station.'

'What do you mean, somewhere near Queen Street Station? Sounds like a mystery. Fuck are you hiding?'

'Nothing,' I snigger. 'Better than going up to Fleetoland though.'

'No doubt.'

'Up for it or not?'

'We'll see,' she goes and starts tampering with her one-tens again; seems to be getting more and more annoyed at the pinkness on her kicking foot. 'What's that stuff called, that you said would shift this blood?'

You won't let them hear 'Crazy Cunt', no, you're working on a poem with more substance, something that'll honour Biscuit. To give him back his voice for a few minutes at least. Would be magic to hear it for real. Words that'll make their ears pop. A poem so sharp that it'll stab their brain. They'll definitely spot themselves in it. But it's their environment that'll be the star of the show. An environment you want to berate. A part of you will need to celebrate it, too. Especially to outsiders who think that it's no better than a hellish sewer. To that, you'll puff your chest out and spout all its glory. Shove it right up their arses. This is your town. It'll never stop being your town. Mibbe in a few weeks, when you're bursting with confidence, you can do one specifically about your town. And when you start reading, the jaws of Vicky Rooney and the others will drop to the floor. After one poem, Nails will see what you've been concealing all this time. She'll understand your inner workings. You never know, listening to all the slammers might ignite that bomb in her; she could try her hand at it. Mibbe Nails can dig out a poem or two about the uber-cuntiness of her dad. She could delve into the fact that she's into lassies and the homophobic shite she's had to deal with her whole life.

You picture the scene: you're standing in front of strangers, giving it laldy with some new poems. Words are flowing. You throw some shapes to accompany them, to bring them to life. They all love what they're listening to;

your insides growl with joy. You want more of that feeling. You begin to see things through your dad's eyes a bit. You've never understood why he loves being up on that stage, flexing his muscles to an audience of randomers. Basking in their praise. In many ways his body is a poem in itself. All that gym work and diet shite is his thinking process and word order, while the competition is when he shows the completed work. You get it. You see him more. Cos you want to see him more.

Headstone

He hasn't surfaced from his scratcher in two days. I've peeked around the door to make sure he hasn't snuffed it in his sleep. Always waiting for the duvet to bob up and down before I leave. The painkillers he took for his napper have floored him, that's the only conclusion for his lazy bastard routine. What else can it be? The worrying thing, for him, is that he's missed about half a dozen gym sessions, not to mention forty-two bland chicken fillets and eighty-six gallons of water. Now, what I know about bodybuilding, you could write on a toenail, but he's got fuck all chance of winning that competition next Saturday. In fact, if he remains holed up in his room, he might not even make it to next Saturday.

Every time my phone pings I jump. Not cos I'm hovering outside Dad's door and want to keep quiet, but cos I always think it's gonna be Trig sniffing about, clarifying plans for Sunday. Can't be doing with the pressure of him sitting on my chest. The ping's a text from Job Centre Plus. Usual pish, no doubt. I read it a few times, then take a screenshot in case I accidentally delete the message.

'You've got to be shittin' me,' I whisper. 'You've got be fuckin' shittin' me,' I say louder. These mad bananas at the Time Capsule have only gone and given me an interview. Me? I mean, why? I'm a series of Nos: No experience. No life-saving skills. No skills. No life. I'd look decent in a pair of red trunks and a yellow vest, that's about it. Fourteen quid an hour though, not too shabby. Above the average rate. I do the calculations in my head. Arithmetic was a skoosh at school, when I could be arsed. Thirty-eight hours at that rate is over five hundred bangers a week. Times four, is over two Gs a month, and that's without overtime. Fuckin' hell's fire! That's loaded material; your golden ticket to freedom, right there. Glad I filled that application form out now. I visualise myself in those red trunks and yellow vest. Hair gelled back. Cutting around the pool's edge, flip-flopping out my nut; the cock of the North. Birds eyeing the fuck out of me. I can see me diving in to save some belter who's sunk to the bottom. Mouth to mouth. Chest pump. Saved. Hero. I feel a tingle in my bones for the first time in yonks. Finally, someone has seen me; willing to hear me and take a chance. If I get this gig, I can burn all my snider gear: the hats, the trackies, the hoodies and the attitude. For all time. Go on a shopping spree for new clobber.

My mouth is dry. Who can I share this info with? I punch the air as though I've scored a postage stamp stoater. If we'd tiles instead of carpets, I'd slide along them; this is

'OK, right,' he goes, and rolls over as though going for another nap.

'Feeling any better?'

He doesn't move. Doesn't say a word. I think he's closed his eyes again. Cheers, Dad, good chat. Let's preserve that unbreakable bond we have.

'How's the head?' I ask him.

The duvet starts riding up and down. But it's not his breathing that's making that movement. I go closer to his side of the bed.

'Dad!'

The duvet's shuddering now, you'd think someone was shaking it.

'Dad!'

I hear him sniffing from under it. Oh, here we go again.

'I'm worried about you,' I go, which is a genuine concern. Mean, you hear about bleeds on the brain days after an attack; could be a serious concussion. Christ, the man could be brain dead by midnight, for all I know. Mibbe I was too hasty thinking he was talking pish.

The duvet is dancing now. Real tears, real emotion. 'Dad!' I say louder. 'I'm worried.'

'Don't worry about me, Connor,' he forces himself to say. 'Honestly, I'm sound, wee man.'

He hasn't called me *wee man* for about five years. Now, I'm worried out my knickers. I go closer, sit on the edge of

243

the bed, put my hand on his shoulder, which feels like a massive, warm watermelon.

'You need to tell me if your head still hurts?' I go. 'Cos if it does, I'll need to phone the doctor or something. You hear about stuff like this all the time.'

He emerges from the duvet and winds his bulky body towards mine.

'Everything hurts.' He wraps his arms around my waist; rests his head on my ribs and starts crying like, well, a wee man. I don't know what to do or say. Do I touch him? Stroke his hair? The sound reminds me of when Mum died. And when Biscuit got murdered. I'm done with tears, man.

'I lied, Connor,' he sniffs.

'About what?'

'Getting jumped the other day.'

'What?'

'Nobody tried to steal my bag.'

I don't want to sound too shocked, or say *Tell me something I don't know*, but I am kinda shocked. Mibbe it's just disappointment. Fuck knows, my head's mangled as well.

'OK, so tell me what happened?' I go, before checking myself. 'But you don't need to tell me if you'd rather not.'

His grip around me tightens. I know he's burying himself into my ribs cos he can't bear to look me in the eye. All these years of him being a dick and now he wants sympathy. Mean, I've a poem to write, an interview to prepare for, a couple of mates to save, and a potential mauling to avoid; an escape route to plan. I've no time for this shite.

'I didn't go to the gym the other day.' He's waiting for me to respond. I don't say a word. I listen. I'm good at that. Best course of action, just ask Nails. 'I went to your mum's grave instead.'

What the ... did I hear that right? He went to ... he actually went to ... he never goes to Mum's grave, neither of us do. What's the fuckin' point? She ain't in there. She's better served in my room, or in my imagination. Another thing, we never speak about Mum or what happened to her. I couldn't even tell you what's written on her headstone, that's how often I've been.

Here lies ... beloved mother of ... wife of ... daughter of ... born ... died ... selfish cunt took a rope to her own neck ... have a gander at Our Lady and say a prayer ... do come again.

This revelation forces me to shift position, and this shift makes me put my palms on his head. His hair's moist.

'Why did you go up there?' I ask.

'Cos I miss her, Connor.'

'I get that.'

'I miss her every day.'

'Aye, me too.'

'I'm lost without her.' He gulps and tries to suck some air in, or swallow the lump in his throat. 'It's been that way since it happened.' I guess time is no healer at all then. Time can fuck off and keep on spinning somewhere else.

'It's OK to feel that way,' I go.

'I should've been there,' he whispers. 'Should've seen the signs.'

'There were no signs to see.' I silently laugh at myself for saying this; I was fourteen, how in the name of fuck would I have known what the signs were. 'That's what everyone says, Dad.'

'I should've helped. Should've been more supportive.'

'But no one knew what she was going through. She hid it, Dad. She hid it all. Even you say that.'

'Or mibbe I was blinded by my own shit at the time. Full of my own selfishness.' I think he's talking to himself here. No use in either agreeing or disagreeing with him, but he may have a point.

'You know it's not your fault, don't you?' I tell him. 'You're not to blame.'

'Most days I feel I am though.'

His tears seem to have stopped, which allows me to shove his frame off me. I manage to slide myself away and at the same time guide his head back onto the pillow. That's when I notice his face is properly bruised. A yellow, purple swelling above his left eye. Looks like a right sore one. So much for frozen sweetcorn.

'That's some shiner you've got.'

He touches the bruise; his face is red and bulging from all that heat and tears. There's a look in his eyes that tells me he's suddenly realised something worse has happened. I'm bursting with a few choice questions.

'So, if nobody tried to steal your bag, how did you get that?' I go, nodding to his eye.

He looks deflated, like in primary school when the teacher shoots down some wee prick who's trying to be a smart cunt in front of the class. Wonder who that was?

'Happened at the graveyard,' he goes.

'Eh?' I feel my face scrunched up with confusion or disgust. Hard to decide which is the dominant one. 'Somebody battered you at the graveyard?' My voice is thon high-pitched way.

'No, nothing like that.'

'Well, what? I'm struggling to understand this, Dad.'

He heaves himself up in the bed. Creaks his neck. Rubs his mouth and nose. Looks like he's just committed a crime. I make my way to the foot of the bed again.

'I was angry, Connor.'

'You're always angry. Big deal.'

'Watch it.'

'Sorry. Finish what you were gonna say.'

He stares at me for ages. I hold my nerve, not letting him win the contest.

'When I went to the graveyard, I was angry. I was standing

in front of your mum's grave and the anger just increased.' He's speaking in a strange monotone, like a horror film villain. 'That's the only emotion I felt. It got really intense.'

'Why were you so angry?'

'Cos she left me.'

'Aye, and me.'

'Cos she left us.' He clears his throat. 'That's why I was angry, no other reason. And I saw red, didn't I?'

'You saw . . . And what . . . what did you do?'

'I attacked her headstone.'

'You what?'

'Punched it. Tried to boot it down, but it wouldn't move.'

'Why the fuck would you do that?' I could feel my own anger rising now.

'It was as if it wasn't me, Connor. Was as if I'd no control of my actions,' he goes. 'You know what I mean by that?'

Do I know what he means? Course I know what he means, lost count of the battles I've been in when I'm out my own body, looking at myself throwing slow-motion haymakers or tearing into some cunt's torso. But it's not me I'm looking at, well, it is me, course it's me, but it feels like someone else has entered my body and I've got no control over what's happening. I'm watching a different person who looks exactly like me. That's what it's like. You don't even feel the pain when you're on the receiving end of a few kicks to the napper, a part of you even enjoys it, that's how bonkers it is.

'Aye, kinda do know what you mean,' I go, still thinking he's off his rocker though. 'But what happened to your head and face?'

'When the headstone wouldn't budge, I started shaking it. Really shaking it. It still didn't shift. So, out of frustration more than anything else, I stuck the head on it a few times.'

'Eh?'

'I stuck the head on it. On the headstone.'

'You fuckin' serious?' I go, face properly scrunched up now, like one of those old drunk gurning cunts.

'That's how I've got this.' He points to his eye.

You don't really know how to process what he's telling you. You can't just slip out and head downstairs to make a cup of tea as if it was a normal day. Your face is stuck in a scream pose. How can you possibly explain to anyone that your old man goes around sticking the nut onto his dead wife's headstone? All this is beyond your knowledge, but, still, you want to suggest he sees someone, a specialist shrink, a person who knows the right thing to do when a man like Dad comes through their doors. But what's the point of speaking to someone? Did it do your mum any good? Not even sure if she was able to speak to anyone, to be honest. The queue's about eight months long anyway. Then it'll be too late. Again. You gaze down at him in that bed, knowing there's fuck all you can do, you've no solutions; you definitely can't look after him. You have to leave him to

249

suffer in his own thoughts. It's a bit like standing on the shore watching someone drown, cos you've no swimming skills, and there's no life ring. You can't walk away so you watch helplessly as they drown to death. It's not my fault I was born into a background like this, but if I stay in it, everything will be my fault.

I want to have a look at that eye, get real close to it, but decide to remain rooted to the floor. He must have some Vallies somewhere, calm him the fuck down, remove madness from his mind for a short while anyway. If I wasn't trying to avoid Trig I could chin him, his brother's bound to have a stash somewhere.

'Dad.'

'What?'

'I don't think you should go near Mum's grave for a while.'

'Don't worry.'

'Some places can be triggering, know what I mean?'

'I've no plans of going back.'

'Christmas and birthdays only.'

He chuckles a bit.

'Aye, I'll bring a gift next time.'

'Can I get you anything? Water? Paracetamol? Tea? A laptop? *Pumping Iron* doc? Valium?' I just add that as a joke, with a sharp dagger attached to it.

'No, I'll be OK. I'll try and sleep. Need to get to the gym in the morning,' he goes. 'And work the morra night.'

I take this as a positive sign, he's getting back on the horse of life. Guy's just feeling a bit sorry for himself, that's all, which is fine, we all need some tears and snotters from time to time. He was probably worried sick in case I found out that he cries like a wean every other night. Should I tell him that genie's out the bottle and nobody cares? He'll need to stop attacking marble stones right enough.

'So you're still doing that competition?' I ask him.

'Aye, but I won't win.'

'It's the taking part that counts.'

'Don't know about that.'

'That's what you used to tell me.'

'Also told you there was a Santa Claus.'

I pause for a second and lean my body towards the bed.

'Telling me that there isn't one?'

'You got nothing to do, Connor?' he goes.

Drawing up a detailed escape plan. Writing a belter of a poem for Sunday. Imagining a world where I can walk freely down the road without being para about some cunt smacking a bottle off my dome. Avoiding all things Trig. No . . . not that much to do.

'Loads,' I tell him.

'Must be tough being double busy.'

Confession

Any other Saturday night I'd be out getting rattled. Stoating about the streets in search of adventure. A laugh at least. Can't be arsed any more. I switch my phone off and sit in my room for most of the night: J Hus, Kendrick and words, no booze, pills or joints. Watching the fort in case Dad comes in from work saying he's been playing head tennis with parked cars. Someone's got to be on frozen veg alert. Got to keep an eye on that one now. What can I say, I'm a changing man.

I try writing something about Mum, or rather *not* having one, but what I vomit onto the page is utterly miserable. As soon as the words leave my mouth, I want to scrape the lump out of my throat with a serrated knife. I'm hoping to get the group to admire me, not take pity on me. Can't be standing up there greetin' into my hands, especially now that I've persuaded Nails to tag along. I made an offer she couldn't refuse: get your cunt kicked in by the Fleeto or scoot around Glasgow in peace and tranquillity with yours truly.

I try one last time with Wee Z.

Wot u up to the morra?

U no wot am up to

Right, enuff of the shite Z

Eh?

Ur no seriously goin with
Trig?

Aye

Me and Nails are headin
into Glasga. Fancy it?

On the blag?

Not exactly. Somethin else

Wot?

Secret

Cant be doin with
secrets Con

*Its no secret that ull get
yer cunt kicked in the
morra if u head up there*

Aye, we'll c, won't we

*Stop acting like the hard
man yer not*

Dots, dots and more fuckin' dots.

*C u next week if ur
around*

If I'M around?

Cunt sends me that googly eye emoji.

Laters

I tried. I fuckin' tried. Back to the words.

My attempt about Biscuit is laughable, even the wee man would be pishin' himself in his grave. *If we had another day, I'd make a change; I'd protect all things within our range.* Sounds like that shite Puff Daddy tune he did about the Notorious B.I.G. Not being big-headed, I prefer my

Notorious Biscuit version. But who wants to write about death? Who wants to hear about death? My world is saturated by it, another thing I can't be arsed with.

I spent an hour or so thinking about Dad and what he did at Mum's grave, and how I might be able to do something creative with that incident. About how he's a tragic figure, how lonely he must feel and how much I actually love the sad, old bastard. That sort of palaver. Thing is, it's easy to *write* that I love him, saying it out loud is a different mindfuck altogether; basically, my mouth dries up and a wee voice in my head prattles *Don't say it, don't say it.* I guess that's how me and Dad roll. Keep it all in. Unless, that is, you reveal that you're desecrating your own wife's grave. Then it's fair game.

I stared out of my window at the high-rise flats. Thirteen floors of junky and jakey heaven; the real forgotten dregs in this town. If it was me living up there, I'd have dived off long ago. Those people in those buildings are fuckin' heroes in my eyes. They take a pounding day after day and still manage to smile at you in the street. They'd give you their last, so they would. That led me into thinking I could mibbe slam about those Tory cunts who constantly lob their two-finger salute grenades at people like us.

Telling you, this poetry lark is no easy ride. PaulaTik, Wee Ginger Archie and the rest of them wrote about what was happening to themselves in the here and now, that's what I need to focus on as well. It's no easy ride at all.

When I switch my phone back on it almost explodes in my hand. You'd think someone's loaded themselves with speed and started battering a glockenspiel, with all the texts ringing in my ear. Trig has only gone and set up a WhatsApp group called *TROOPS*. Fuckin' magic! He sends about twenty-seven messages, all saying a different version of the same thing.

Right boyz Im well geared up fur the morra

Am fuckin' buzzin

Just gonna do a bucket here an watch conor mcgregor on youtube

Thats us tooled-up. Got all the bricks sorted they look minted solid as fuck

Meet at mine around 12

Wit do u say Con boy?

Meet at the westend bar
if uz prefer

Nae swallying the night
U want ur head straight
fur the morra

Am ready to do time for
that yobboy cunt

Nae blades . . . aye that
will be right. Wink!
Wink!

You fuckin' there Con?

Watch each others
backs right?

Whos up for a bottle the
morra night?

Am gonna get MWI
when we get back

Wee Z and Nails just add a few *ayes* and *no bothers* in

between Trig's ramblings. He's got no idea that I'll be a definite no-show; hopefully the other two will be as well. I feel a bit ashamed for not standing up to the cunt and telling him that I want heehaw to do with it. I know it's a cowardly way of dealing with Trig, but, honestly, I can't be doing with his aggro. Or the need to explain myself. Not the day. Not any day. I don't need to justify my decisions to anyone, least of all that bawbag.

I send Nails a message away from the *TROOPS* group.

Meet me at the Sunnyside
for the 9.25. Don't be late.

I knock the phone off again after she sends a thumbs-up emoji reply. Can't beat a bit of original thinking.

Talking of which ... I can always fall back on 'Crazy Cunt' if I can't engage my brain, but that's the last thing I want to do; can't have Trig on my mind when I'm up there. I've a solid idea of what I want to spout. Me and Biscuit used to riff all the time about this godforsaken shithole of a town; the place that's moulded me into who I am today. We'd spit lyrics about the shiteness of the area; play daft wee rap battles. His were always better than mine. It was him who told me what exactly a Treacle Town was, made loads of sense the way he put it. *Is it possible to escape where you're from and remain in it at the same time? Or is that just called contentment and happiness?* Think the only escape I actually need is from the person I became, the person I was. Thon fuckin' empty-headed dunce Ned (it's OK for me to say it). If I can do that then that's real freedom right there.

Fuck knows why, but I reach behind my bed and pull out the bag Biscuit's mum gave me. I sit staring at what's inside for ages; it peeks back at me like the memory of a dead friend. Two items: I touch them. There's something sad about them, not emotionally sad. Pathetic sad. As if I'm looking into a mirror of the past, a past I no longer recognise. A past that needs to get launched. Do I bin what's in this bag or use it as inspiration? Looking inside, I can't feel what Biscuit's mum wanted me to feel. I'm not like her, he didn't come out of me, he's not my creation, so I can't keep hold of him forever, not in the same way she will. Oh, he'll be with me, no danger of that, but he won't fuck with my state of mind nor stop me from spreading my wings. There'll be no giant photo on my wall; eyes following me around the room. The wee man will understand this. I'd want him to discard me in the same way.

I squish away at the bag again.

Has to be done. The wait's been too long. The fear. I take the first thing out and bring it up to my nose. Crush my face into it. Use it to dab my eyes. Might be my imagination fuckin' with me, but I can smell the reek of him. I was there when he bought it. Fifteen smackers. Not cheap. Celtic shop across from Asda. I was mad jealous. He didn't bag it, just put the beanie straight on his napper and sauntered out of the shop. Gallus as fuck. Black wool, emerald green badge on the front. It was a belter. He wore that thing until the badge's glow dimmed. I follow the shape of the badge with my fingers, tracing the four-leaf clover a few times. Some luck that brought him. I shove the beanie on my dome and take out item number two. Never seen it in my puff before. A shiny notebook, the size of a novel. Hardcover. I flick the pages. Packed with words until halfway through, then some doodles, but mostly blank. I read. Some words and phrases I recognise from back in the day. I keep shaking my head and whispering '*Fuck sake*,' to myself. The secretive wee cunt, who knew?

I read it again and again. Never once taking the Celtic beanie off.

I stick J Hus off and type *How to succeed at interviews* into a YouTube search. As if it's gonna get me the Time Capsule gig. What pops up is a selection of nauseating Yanks trying to get sales and banking jobs. The basic take home: don't act like a dick, shake hands and look cunts in the eye when they're talking to you, and, finally, don't dress as if you've just done a twelve-hour shift on the bin lorries. I go old school and fire up Public Enemy's *It Takes a Nation of Millions to Hold Us Back* in the hope that the beats and words seep right into my brain and inspire the life out of me. Eventually I pick up my pen again and write the first line just to see how it looks in my style. *His* first line:

> *Treacle Town, you made us fear, tear, battle, bottle*
> *for everything we have.*

Finally conked around two, and wake as the birds are tweeting. Sevenish. My stomach is a swirl of anxiety, knocking lumps out of everything else surrounding it. I stare at the ceiling and take in long Wim Hof puffs of air; gulping it into my lungs in the hope that it swamps the anxiety. If there was ever a need for some top-quality Vallies, this was it. I pick up my phone and put sweaty thumbmarks all over the screen; shite scared to turn it back on cos I know what's about to land. And I'm not wrong, like a detonation in my fuckin' hand. Mr Glockenspiel has popped in to see me this morning. Naturally, Trig has done a fuckin' Uzi spray of texts. Most written after sucking his bucket, it seems:

> *fuckin' love u shower of*
> *cunts*
>
> *conor mcgregors got*
> *some patter on him*
> *cunts a pure howl*

feel like the morra im
goin into battle with my
bros

Wit happens stays in
the streets no fuckin'
rats no grasses

Im totally melted

where r u cunts?

aye well it's late

see uz the morra
outside westend bar
don't be late

signin aff fur the night

luv u cunts no joke
aboot it

lets do it fur Biscuit
boys

After reading every message I sigh heavier and louder; feel a bit sick. Sick that I'm letting down a mate; worse than a grass. Abandoning a mate on the battlefield; worse than anything. But he's been told how mad it is. Not my fault if the dick doesn't listen. It'll be fine. When he realises that he's flying solo, he'll slink home, have a roll and tattie scon, curse the fuck out of us and get mangled on Sean's shite super skunk. He'll simmer down soon enough. By Tuesday afternoon we'll be reduced to being a gaggle of shitebags and nothing more. We'll all move on. What's he gonna do? Want a square go with each of us in turn? No danger of that, Nails would knock him into next week.

I send Nails a reminder message, then tell her to switch off her phone. I read through my poem again. Three times. A tweak here, a tweak there. First step's the hardest, so they say. Each step after that and the treacle thins, and well, it's all plain sailing from then on. Soon I'll be floating, apparently.

Dad's sinking a litre of water in the kitchen when I get downstairs. Don't know why I was tiptoeing. Just presumed he was sleeping off a night of bouncing.

'I didn't hear you come down,' I go.

'Early gym session.'

'That's good.' I give him a genuine smile cos it's a weight off my mind. He starts guzzling the water again like an escaped prisoner. 'Feeling better then?' I point to his eye, which resembles the colour of a squished chip.

'Aye, much better,' he goes, wiping his mouth dry. I've a feeling he's not talking about his eye.

'So, you're definitely still gonna compete then?'

'I don't like quitters, capiche? And anyway, it's the taking part that counts.' He tilts his head knowingly. So do I. We both laugh. I could hug him, but no danger. I stand my ground a couple of yards away and keep my grin.

'You better get some good bronzer for that eye,' I tell him.

'I'll get Big Linda to work her magic on it.'

'You know we're all coming, don't you? Me, Wee Z and Nails.'

'No pressure then.' He fans his hands like he's being held up. He clocks my old school backpack. Carrying nothing but my notebook and pen. 'Going somewhere?'

'Into Glasgow,' I tell him as though it's an everyday occurrence. He raises the squished chip's brow.

'What's happening in the big smoke?'

The way he's gawking at me, I know he's thinking I'm off on the blag with the troops. Whatever. His expression changes, definitely believing that I'm off to cause carnage somewhere; I've seen that change a thousand times. Mibbe this is my opportunity to come clean, test the waters of telling him I've joined a poetry group. He'd probably be raging if I did, thinking I was taking the pish right out of him. *Don't stand there and take me for some stupid cunt, Connor.*

'Just heading in with Nails.'

'Aye, but for what?' He pushes further, suspicion dripping from his jaws. You can hardly blame the man for having trust issues. My best mate murdered. Police visits galore. Practically booted out of school. Chasing my tail every other day and trying to stave off boredom. Stoned, pished, or both most weekends. Hardly the model child. 'Simple question, Connor.'

'Just going for a gander around some shops,' I go.

'No you're not.' He steps closer, not nose-to-nose stuff, but close enough for me to smell him. Who the fuck still wears Brut? 'I know you're lying.' He glares right through me. I take a wee step back, out of his reach at least. Fuck him, and his bulk.

'OK,' I go. 'You really want to know where I'm going?'

'Wouldn't be asking otherwise, would I?'

I swipe my tongue around my front teeth, loop an arm through my backpack and sling it over my shoulder. My teeth taste metallic; same way after doing acid. This is one of those genie-out-the-bottle moments. Fuck it! Who cares? There's no crime being committed here.

'Well?' he goes.

'Well . . . I kinda . . . joined this club in Glasgow.'

'What club?'

'It's based at the Royal Conservatoire of Scotland.'

Now, if you want to see confusion on someone's coupon,

just chuck the word 'conservatoire' into the conversation and it'll show up like a dodgy tenner under a UV light.

'What club?' he asks again.

I stare him squarely in the eyes, straighten myself up and puff my chest out.

'It's a kinda street rap thing.' The look of confusion doesn't leave him. 'Poems and stuff.'

For disbelief, shock and doubt, just chuck in the word 'poems', as well. He drops the water bottle to his side and smacks the lid shut with the palm of his hand. A grin develops on his chops; I can make out his gnashers.

'If you start laughing, I'm just gonna walk,' I tell him. 'Am no joking.'

'I'm not laughing,' he goes. You can see his wee brain going into overdrive; he's no clue of what to say. 'Poems? What like Robert Burns?'

'Aye, poems. And not Robert Burns,' I spit. 'And, anyway, there's nothing wrong with Robert Burns. Mum used to read me one of his about this wee beastie when I was a wean.'

'That right?'

'Aye, it was good. She'd put on a mad accent doin' it. Not remember?'

'Wasn't my thing,' he goes.

'Well, your loss.'

He nods his head and relaxes his body.

'So, how does this poem thing work then?'

'Well, it's not like the poetry you did at school, we don't sit around and write essays about poems. It's more like street poetry.'

'Street—'

'They call it slam.' He's nonplussed, pure gawking at me; flummoxed out his nut. 'Like rapping.'

'O-Kay.'

'But not rapping the way Snoop or Nas rap, know what I mean?'

'Aye, but not really.'

'A bit like hip-hop meets poems.'

'Hip-hop meets poems?'

'Fuckin' hell, it's like being inside an echo chamber,' I go. 'We write our own stuff and read it in front of the rest of the group. It's as popular as anything.'

'Poetry reading then?'

'No, Dad. We don't read. It's called slam. We write stuff that's happening in our lives, or stuff we've got strong opinions about and read them aloud. That's it.' You'd think I was telling him that I was off to join the Army. 'Actually, you don't just read it, you kinda perform it,' I go, moving my hands around as if I'm actually performing. 'They call it performance poetry.'

'So not slam then?'

Am I in my kitchen or in the polis station?

'No, it *is* slam, but it's also performance poetry.'

'Are you taking the piss, Connor?'

'No, I'm not. Look, performance poetry and slam are basically the same thing. I'm just using both terms cos that's my understanding of it.' He nods his head the way the plod do when they've been told, *No officer, I haven't been drinking*. 'Dad, it's my first time going, so I'll be finding out more about it. It might be shite. Might be decent. Who knows. Just trying something new. Something different.'

At this, Dad starts pishin' himself laughing. He joke-punches me on the shoulder. His joke-punches leave bruises, by the way.

'Course I know what slam is,' he goes. 'You think I'm a thick bastard?'

'No, just—'

'I've heard you listening to it on YouTube—'

'Eh?'

'And I've heard you do your own stuff. You thought I didn't know, didn't you?'

I shrug and feel a wave of humiliation creep up from my one-tens. Talk about morto. 'You've a voice like a foghorn, Connor, even when you're whispering.'

Fuck sake! Is nothing sacred these days?

'Fuck sake! Is nothing sacred these days?' I go.

He lifts his hand to my shoulder, which makes me flinch. He rests it on me, his fingers snaking down onto the top of my back.

269

'I hate saying it, but it sounded good,' he goes. 'I'm not lying to you.'

'Really?'

'The bits I heard, anyway. It did. It sounded really good.'

'Right, well, glad you liked it.'

'What time's this poetry thing at?'

'Half-ten. But I'm meeting Nails at Sunnyside at half-nine.'

He flicks a wrist and his Fitbit springs into action.

'Well, you better get your arse in gear then,' he goes and removes his paw from my shoulder.

For a split I think he's about to hug me; it's the perfect moment after all. Just a wee body bump one, a bro slap on the back. Nothing more. I loop my other arm into the backpack and heave it up. Feels like I'm heaving air, there's heehaw in that bag. Except a notebook full of words. And, mibbe, my dignity.

Con-Serve-A-Twar

My leg's been vibrating since we got off the train; forgot to put my phone off. Still early, so Trig's red mist won't have descended just yet. He'll be texting me from his kip. I'll turn the thing off before we go in.

'How the fuck do you pronounce that?' Nails goes, staring up at the sign and trying to mouth it, sounding out each syllable as if she's just new at this reading lark.

'Conservatoire,' I tell her. 'It's a w sound after the t.'

'Eh?' she goes. 'Speak the Queen's, Con.'

'Technically it's the King's now,' I go.

Nails gives me ice-cold eyes.

'Aye, well, technically I don't give a fuck.'

'Twar.' I frown at her. 'Con ... serve ... a ... twar.' She looks at me as if I'm speaking German or something. 'Mean, it's not that hard to pronounce.'

'Aye, cos you can't get moving for conserva-whatevers where we're from,' she sniggers. Credit where credit's due, she's a funny cunt at times. 'So this is it? This is where all the poetry poofs hang out?'

'That's it.'

'There's no way I'm doing poems and stuff, Con,' she goes. 'If they ask me to read anything, I'm bolting.'

'Bolting to where?' I go. 'To give Trig handers?'

When we hopped onto the train, Nails was a bag of cats in case any other young teams were heading into Glasgow, so to shift her fear focus I had to tell her about where we were going, had to get her on that train first though; too scared to say anything on the platform so she couldn't tell me to ram my Sunday morning poetry sesh up my arse. No place to hide on a train. Initially I wanted to rock up to the Royal Conservatoire of Scotland and hit her with the news outside the main doors. Aw, well. It had to be done between Garrowhill and Shettleston. Once I explained that all she had to do was sit on her hole and watch people reading, then it was fine. I sealed the deal when I pulled up some stuff on YouTube. Nails's two key concerns after that were: *Will they ask me to read?* And, *Any fit birds gonna be there?* I'd worried myself into sleepless nights about anyone finding out, but I needn't have bothered. Telling her was the easy part. She seemed genuinely excited about hearing people read. Mibbe she's just excited about a day out, or blanking Trig.

I'm glad she's with me. My mate. As a soon as that whiff of polish hits my nose, I know I couldn't have stepped inside this building without someone close to me. Asking her was a hunner per cent the right decision. Shame about Wee Z, but I can't carry everyone's worries on my shoulders; hope he's safe though. The pair of us stand in the main foyer doing three-sixties on the heels of our one-tens. Loads of stairs lead to God knows where, tonnes of glass everywhere, pictures of famous Scottish actors all over the walls.

'What is it they do here?' Nails goes, as if she's that little tadger Charlie, inside the Chocolate Factory. Mean, it's only a building, a notch up from a school. Nothing special. Well, a wee bit special for us. Still, only bricks and glass at the end of the day.

'Acting and stuff,' I tell her.

'All this for pretending to be someone else?'

'Studio five's down here,' I whisper. 'C'mon.'

I honestly thought that my heart would be pounding out my chest, but I'm calm. Better in this building than on Fleeto streets, eh? I touch my phone, a ticking time bomb in my pocket, and wonder what Trig's up to at twenty-five past ten. My guess, he's applying varnish to the Millwall bricks. All lined up on his kitchen table like infantry ready to go over the top.

Vicky Rooney's standing at the door as we approach. When she clocks me, her smile runs from ear to ear.

'Connor, is it?' she goes.

'Aye . . . I mean, yes.'

'Oh, I'm so glad you made it,' she says, and puts out her hand for me to shake. Her hand's like smooth twigs.

'Welcome.' She peeks over my shoulder. 'And you've brought a friend, I see.'

'Aye … Erm … this is erm, Jodie.' I almost forget what her name is; been that long since I've used or heard it. School, probably. Feels a wee bit embarrassing or weird saying it aloud. 'This is my pal. She's just gonna watch, if that's OK?'

'Of course it is. The more the merrier,' Vicky Rooney goes. 'Come on, the rest of the group are already here.' As we saunter in, Vicky Rooney whispers in my lughole, 'It's perfectly fine to say "aye," you know. All language, dialect and localisms are accepted here, Connor.' I nod nervously and enter the studio, my mate shimmying behind like a lap dog.

The full monty are here: Ginger Archie, who's not as wee as I once thought, and actually not as ginger. Better get a new name for the geezer. PaulaTik, who, let's be honest, is an absolute belter. Her head's buried in her notebook; takes this stuff seriously. The Stone Islanders from the train shift their eyes in my direction as if to say, *I know that cunt from somewhere.* I'm delighted to have the bold Nails by my side. Toni D, who looks as comfortable as a fart without an arse, a nailbiter. There's a few others I've never seen in my puff before. Vicky Rooney asks us all to sit in a wee semicircle. So, we all sit as though we're part of the AA's youth wing.

'Before we start, I'd just like to welcome Connor and Jodie,' she goes.

Everyone says in unison *'Awright.'* Me and Nails share a grin.

'Welcome to our group.' Vicky Rooney then tells everyone that, 'They've all come from Coatbridge,' before looking at us again. 'Is that right?'

'Aye,' we go together, and sit a bit taller.

I scan the room to gauge reactions to Coatbridge. A few frowns and turned-down mouths have been duly noted. Vicky Rooney casts her eyes around the horseshoe.

'Connor?' she goes.

'Aye?' OK, I might be forcing far too many 'ayes' out.

'Did you manage to bring anything for us to hear?'

Every eye in the studio burns a hole in my head. Even Nails looks excited.

'I did bring something, aye,' I go.

'Fabulous.' Vicky Rooney claps her hands together. 'Mibbe you'd like to read it to us.' She points to a kinda performing area in one of the corners. Instantly, I want it to swallow me into its darkness.

'No bother,' I go as though this *is* no bother for me. I'm shittin' breezeblocks while rummaging through my backpack. 'I didn't memorise it, is that OK?'

'Of course it is,' Vicky Rooney says.

As I'm walking towards the performance area, I do a few Wim Hofs. Nails shouts, 'On yersel, Con.' People snigger, I guess she breaks an awkward silence.

When I'm in position, I turn and find them all on the edge of their seats. Ginger Archie has his elbows on his knees, in deep concentration. PaulaTik has her arms folded in a kinda *This better be worth my fuckin' attention* manner. Toni D seems as scared as me; she's probably up next. The Stone Islanders don't give a rat's arse, just as long as I'm worse than them.

I open Biscuit's shiny notebook to the page. Take a deep one. *Here goes, wee man.*

'I wish I could tell you that I wrote this myself, but I didn't.' Some faces squint their confusion. Vicky Rooney raises two eyebrows … I'm here doing my *enjoyment and participation* bit, know what I mean? 'This is from a poet called Mark McVitie. You won't have heard of him.' I stare at Nails, her eyes are as wide as the ghost emoji, the rest just look perplexed. 'Mark was my mate. He's not able to be here today, so I'm going to read it for him, if that's OK?' Everyone nods. Everyone.

I puff out, look down at the page, see his face smiling up from it. Hear his words: *On yersel, Con. Do me proud. Gee it laldy, ma man.* 'It's a poem about where we come from.' I nod to Nails. 'Where Mark came from.' You could hear a pin drop. 'It's called "Treacle Town".' Nails gives me a subtle thumbs up. Vicky Rooney fires a grin of approval. If it goes down like a bottle of puke, it's all his fault. One more Wim

Hof, and fuck it, here goes nothing. 'Treacle Town, you made us fear, tear, battle, bottle for everything we have.'

Doesn't matter if they were Biscuit's words, you feel elated. Delighted. Exhilarated. All those types of words. That was better than any joint you've had. Better than winning a battle. That's the thoughts running through your head while washing your hands. You look at your reflection in the toilet mirror. You've done something decent for once. Something good. And fucked nobody off in the process. No one's ever applauded you like that or slapped you on the back with that many congratulations. You feel as though a new person is staring back at you. A better person. After splashing water on your sweaty face, you open your eyes. And there she is, standing right behind you. You knew she'd come today.

Hiya, son.

Mum!

I'm beyond proud, you know that?

Didn't think I was capable of it.

You're capable of anything you want to be.

Thanks.

You're going to make it, Connor, love. You're going to make it.

I hope so.

And the best bit is that you're going to make it all on your own. On your own terms. In your own voice. Your own heart.

That's what I want more than anything, Mum.

It's out there, all you need to do is go get it.

I think I can see it; almost touch it.

It's all I've ever wanted for you, son.

Do you still want me to come with you?

There's no need now.

Why?

Because you've found it.

What?

Whatever you've been looking for. It's right in front of you.

Everything is yours. Your own path. Go walk it.

Texts

It's not until we reach Queen Street around half-three that I switch my phone back on, making sure to click the silent button. Ten seconds max until my leg starts shuddering like it's receiving electric shock treatment. Nails sidles up to me on the platform and whispers in my ear: 'That was fuckin' bangin', Con. Seriously, mate, I was well impressed. I know it was Biscuit's, but it's the best cover version I've heard in my puff.'

She punches my shoulder. I chuckle.

'Coming back, then?'

'I'll think about it. Depends on my training.'

'You could always do one yourself,' I go. 'Something about ... you know ... lassies and that.' Nails winces, looks at me as though I'm talking absolute flaps.

'Who the fuck cares about that shite, Con?'

'Aye, right enough.'

'I might do one about kicking the shit out of my da, though,' she winks.

'Not a bad idea,' I go, but obviously she's as serious as a wrestling match. 'How's he doing anyway?'

'Got his stitches out yesterday. Concussion lasted a couple of days. Ego still bruised to fuck though.'

'Whose wouldn't after a bleaching from your daughter?'

Nails laughs, but looks slightly embarrassed at the same time.

'Cunt hasn't said boo to a goose since,' she goes. 'So, happy days.'

'Yer maw OK?'

'She's sorted. What is it they call it again?'

I shrug my ignorance.

'A survivor,' Nails remembers. 'She's surviving.'

'Aren't we all.'

I step towards the edge of the platform and think about that thing: what if I jumped when a train comes? Or, better, what if I nudge some spangle onto the tracks and watch the train run over them. Tempting. When the train pulls up, I walk back to Nails and we get on at a four-seater.

'Have you checked yer phone?' she asks. I shake my head, which is a lie cos mine has already vibrated to near-explosion. I know what to expect.

'No, me neither.'

'Check it.'

Nails takes hers out and switches it on; her messages sound like a bullet being fired, and I'm in line of fire.

'Read them, they're all on the WhatsApp,' Nails goes. 'Guy's lost it.'

We start reading as the train pulls out of Queen Street. No words spoken. No words needed.

> *Thats five past where r*
> *u cunts?*

> *?????*

> *Ur no pickin up yer fon*

> *All yer fons r off*

> *TURN THEM ON*

> *Even wee zs here*

> *Im standing here way a*
> *bag of tools u better*
> *move yer holes*

> *If yer no here by 20*
> *past am goin up there*
> *masel*

FUCK R YOOZ?

Shitebags

Fuckin shite bags

Biscuit will be fuckin
greetin in his grave

Shitebag cunts

Me an wee z will show
you how its done

Ill tell Yobboy you all
shat it when am kickin
his cunt in

Am gonna knock fuck
out yeez when i see
yeez ya bunch of fuckin
shitebag bitches

Fuckin rats no better
than fleeto cunts worse
in fact

Am coming for you
hoors

Pair of you r dead no
fuckin danger aboot it

I'd be lying if I said those messages didn't rattle me. But I'll tell you one thing, that mad swally merchant is barking up the wrong fuckin' tree if he thinks he can threaten me. No danger I'll be living in fear of him. So, if he wants that to be the case then let's have it. Let's go to town.

'If he comes anywhere near me,' Nails goes, 'I'll break his fuckin' fingers.'

'Trig's full of pish, you should know that by now.'

'Then there's that mad brother of his as well,' Nails goes.

For the rest of the journey, we sit in our own thoughts. I watch the Eastend of Glasgow whizz past. Lean my head against the window and follow the miserable shops, the unfit housing, the decay of everywhere, the people milling around without a bean to their name; the absolute sadness and pointlessness of it all. Not as much as a football pitch or swing park for miles. Honestly, if this is the modern, progressive Scotland, then they can shove it right up their hole; mibbe they'll find some politicians up there. Those cunts should hang their heads in shame, the shitehole they've turned this country into.

My head clatters against that glass and I think to myself: thank fuck I don't live in any of these parts. When the train pulls away from Easterhouse, I'm delighted to be heading home to Coatbridge. The Brig. A genuine kip it might be, but it's my genuine kip, a genuine kip with community spirit, and much less of a kip than the kips I've just passed.

There's no buzz about us when you get off the train. Any excitement about the slam group has been left on the streets of Glasgow. Here, in the Brig, you sense something in the air, more than your usual Sunday silence. Usually at this time there'll be a crew of Celtic fans milling around after an early afternoon kick-off. Steamin', chanting, swigging half-deckers of Buckie. Now, nothing. An eerie hush. Funny smell hovering about, too. You can taste it. You have to smack your tongue on the top of your mouth. Mibbe you're imagining it, but you don't think so. You've always had a really good sense of pending danger.

We walk home, avoiding the obvious chat about Trig. Nails's talking about ramping up her training regime and trying to get lottery funding. I want to tell her about my interview at the Time Capsule on Friday, but don't want to brag, or jinx myself. At the bottom of the hill, from the station, we stop at the fork in the road. Separation time. Definitely something funny in the air.

'Cheers for coming,' I go.

'No bother.'

'Thought it was gonna be shite, but it was actually OK,' Nails goes. 'Right.' She starts to head in one direction. 'Catch you during the week.'

'Sound,' I go.

'Magic,' she goes.

'Don't forget my dad's competition next Saturday,' I shout after her. 'I've got tickets for you and Wee Z.'

The fear is setting in, I can feel it.

She gives a thumbs-up and heads off; so do I.

'Con!' Nails shouts after me. I stop, turn.

'Aye?'

'You did him proud, you know.'

'Who?'

'Biscuit.'

I don't know what to say, so I shrug.

I wave her off again and instantly feel a thump in the pit of my stomach. Can't explain it. That taste is back as well. It stays with me all the way home.

As soon as the door opens, he's there waiting for you. Standing. Not in his bouncer pose. No aggressive arms folded. There's a softness to his face. His eye looks much better. Brighter. Sparklier. Christ almighty, has he been at the greetin' again? Your heart hasn't stopped racing all day.

'Everything awright, Dad?'

'You were in Glasgow, Connor, right?' he goes.

I look confused, cos I am.

'Aye,'

'All day?'

'All day, aye. How?'

'Do you have witnesses?'

'Plenty. Nails. Loads of other people. CCTV in Queen Street, Buchanan Street, Nike shop.' He nods his head; I know by his eyes that he believes me. 'Why do I need witnesses?'

'You sent any text messages to anyone today about anything?' My heart feels like it's trying to burst out of my chest. I could be a hip-hop beat. My breathing is shallow.

'No. How?' Dad moves towards me and reaches out a hand. 'Dad, what's happened?' My voice is croaky, shaky. Fearing the worst. His hand rests on my shoulder.

But you know.

You already knew.

You've known since you got off the train.

'You better come and sit down, son.'

Son?

Fuck!

I knew.

I just knew.

Trig

Trig's da doesn't need anyone to hold him up. He doesn't strike me as a man who does public bawling; no squealing like a banshee for this big man. That's a given. Sean just sits in the pew staring at his polished shoes. Can't polish a turd . . . Prick! Even so, the scene still scuds you full force in the chops. I look around. Denise clocks me, her daggers are less sharp this time. Mibbe she pities me? She's not the worst, that one, always said it. She even manages to give Nails a sort-of friendly grin. No sign of Biscuit's old dear, would probably bring back too many bad memories.

The look on our faces is sadness, and guilt. Guilt that Wee Z can't be here. Guilt that he's still lying in a hospital bed; he'll survive, although his cricket career might've taken a dunt. His right hand was severed trying to protect his head from machete blows. Better a hand than an artery, I suppose. He got off lightly, it was Trig they wanted; the grand prize.

Guilt is throttling me cos I could've tried harder to save him, to have been a better mate, to not have abandoned him. What's done is done. Here we are again. Yet again. And yet again I'd fuck all to do with it. One thing hasn't changed: I still have this mad desire to bawl and splatter the contents of my throat all over the altar.

The sight and sound in the chapel is similar to Biscuit's. That noise of a preventable death swooning around like a ghost. All my memories are being stoked. If I could go through life without hearing that noise again, I'd die a happy man. But there's no chance of that, is there?

Tell you one thing, I don't mind turning on the waterworks in front of all these people; tears blur my vision. The coffin's just a smear below the huge crucifix. High on the cross, Christ is all fuzzy until I blink him back into twenty-twenty. Salt water falls onto my cheek. Nails sees me wiping it away. She tightens her mouth as if to say, *It's OK, my man, I understand.* But these tears aren't Trig's alone, they're for them all: Mum, Biscuit, friendships, youth.

The echoes of Biscuit's mum screaming, *That's my boy in there. That's my boy* still ring in the air. Who's gonna scream for Trig? Not his da. Not his brother.

Trig, my one-time mate. Our one-time mucker. Once, one of the lads. In that box. Now it's his turn to be wearing a crisp shirt and dark tie like a flute player in a Republican band. He'd like that. Right enough, he could've been wearing his Kenzo trackie. I never saw; they couldn't open the coffin cos his face was carnage. No one knew if he was peaceful or adorable. Four times, they got him. Chest twice. Once in the shoulder. Belter on the face. On the face! Couldn't have a coffin open in that state, you'd give cunts nightmares. You can't unsee shit like that.

Unlike at Biscuit's, there were no big crowds of people to squeeze past. Prayers at his gaff was a small ramble: us two, a few neighbours, some relatives and the priest. Not many people knew the rosary, we all kinda mumbled along. You could tell that Sean wanted to kick fifty shades of shite out of us, he was rippin', pure mad for it; eyeing us all night. You can put on a wager that we're on his *Some cunt's goin' to get fuckin' leathered when this is all over* list. Sean won't let this go, no danger, revenge is in his family's DNA.

Not as much as a triangle sandwich on show. Tea and soggy digestives was your lot. My expectations weren't high.

I was glad the coffin was shut, couldn't be doing with those images again. I touched his wee gold nameplate: Liam Gunn, date of birth, date of death, and the classy *You'll never walk alone* engraved underneath. I couldn't help thinking of the irony of that engraving, cos that's exactly what he did. Forget Wee Z, Trig walked alone. And if he hadn't, he'd still be here.

In a silent moment, when I was sure no one was looking, I clutched the side of the coffin and willed him back to life; at the very least I wanted to see him one last time. I needed to tell him that I was sorry I let him down, but also to cane the cunt for not listening to reason. What fuckin' eejit doesn't listen to reason? All I could do was bend down and give the coffin a kiss; that taste of wood and varnish coated my mouth. Then the choir in my heart piped up. 'I'll miss you Trig, I will. It didn't need to end like this. Sleep well, bud,' I whispered.

His da was sunk on a chair in the corner. No big thing, that was his go-to position. I didn't want to speak to him, but it was pretty unavoidable. The two of us shuffled over, Nails tugging at my jacket like a wean holding on to their mum. My face was matted with shame. Legs like liquid. He must've known that we were heart sorry about what happened. How could he not? Beyond sorry, devastated. He barely looked up. I think he was half-pished. Then he asked me in a croaky voice: 'You'll come to the Bank Social Club after the mass, won't you?'

There's zero options open, you can't refuse. Not when your mate is lying in a box in the corner of the room. I looked at Nails. Nods aplenty.

'Aye, no bother, Mr Gunn,' Nails went.

'We'll have a good swally to our Liam, eh, boys?' He then gazed off into the distance again.

To this day I see Trig decked out in our school football team's strip. Cheeky grin, wonky teeth. Freckles. Barnet gelled down against his forehead. We all had that same look. A midfield general. Loved a dribble. Solid in any tackle. Found a pass too. Two-footed. He wasn't a bad player, could've played at a higher level if he'd put the work in. Pure lazy bastard though.

Dad had to look out the Crombie coat again. That's now three times I've seen him in it. He's next to me, arms tightly folded; I feel safe against his muscles. Against him. He knows it wasn't my fault. I can sleep at night knowing that I'm not responsible for what happened to Trig. I wasn't even there. I told them everything I did that day, which was backed-up by various people. Same as Nails.

Being here again is sore. Another one lost. I can sense venom in people's eyes when they look at us; to them, we'll never change. Always those hopeless Ned cunts with fuck all going for us. A no brainer that one of us will be next. There's a poem in it.

Trig's uncle adjusts the wee mic.

'In thanking you for the life of Liam, we ask you, Lord, to accept the good things he has done. And that you may lead him, in your mercy, to eternal life.'

The exact same meaningless words that came out of my mouth at Biscuit's.

If it was up to me, I'd have said something like:

Trig was one troubled soul. He didn't have the support that many of us take for granted. Even though we were growing apart and taking our own paths in life, I always saw him as one of my best mates. I'll always think that. And, like the rest of us, he had his dreams and desires. It's a tragedy that he won't get to do them now.

'Lord hear us,' Trig's uncle says, leaning into the mic.

'Lord graciously hear us,' everyone goes in return.

'Walk With Me, Oh My Lord', that's the hymn that got me at Biscuit's, and that's the song that gets us here too. The hymn they carry the coffin out the chapel to. Unsurprisingly, we weren't asked to lend a shoulder. As soon as it kicks in there's not a dry eye in the chapel. I've this strong desire to scream at the top of my lungs. I glance at Nails. Wish Wee Z was here. A huge bit of me wants to hug them. Something tells me that this might be the last time we see each other for a while. Dunno why. Just a feeling.

When the coffin passes, I think what mine will look like when it's my turn. Hopefully not as tacky as Biscuit's and not as cheap-looking as Trig's. And hopefully not for fuckin' donkey's years.

My shift at the Time Capsule started at one, so I couldn't make the afters at the Bank Social Club. Apparently, I didn't miss anything.

Dad didn't win. But that's not what's important.

Capiche?

Treacle Town

Treacle Town, you made us fear, tear, battle, bottle
for everything we have.
You're a hard bastard.
A tough nut.
A swinging hook.
A bruising uppercut.

Treacle Town, why do you have to make life so difficult?
Street after street, a dizzying kaleidoscope of
takeaways, Turkish barbers and tanning salons.
A life prefixed with NO.
Graffiti
Balls
King
Pope
Heroes
Hope.

Treacle Town, you've given us zero
                              chance of growing older.
Death in youth
A bang-average diet,
aye, something cheap for the sweet tooth.

Do you hate us with such venom?
Are we that bleak, hopeless, weak?
Do we have anything redeemable, or is
                              it simply too late?
Is living here our luckless slice of fate?

Treacle Town, would a couple of decent restaurants
have been too much to ask?
A chainless coffee shop; some belter bespoke gaff,
as the rest have.
C'mon, give us a town like theirs ... but keep our spirit:
They have country parks
We have the railway lines.
They have woods
We have disused steel works.
They have gyms with plunge pools
We have online casinos.
Bookshops
Vape shops
Colleges
Chapels
Posh Cars
Windowless bars.
They have bonny roads and weans that do elocution.
We have human decay, a sight pollution.

Treacle Town, I'll tell you one thing,
Retail parks and rotten housing ain't no solution.

Treacle Town, I've run through your every scheme
Walked your every street
Toured the town centre
Rain, hail, sleet, heat.
You're everything
and nothing.
My prison
I hate you
I do.
You make me want better; want to be better.
But, without you I could never have been
                    anything but better.

Treacle Town, you're Airdrie, Alloa, Cumnock,
                    Coatbridge:
Dream town nightmare town.
Both at the same time town
High and low town
Down down down town
Drink, drugs and deficient town
You're all heart town
Soft-shell town

Beauty on the inside town.
My friend
My home
My saviour.

Treacle, I fuckin' love you, Town.

Mark 'Biscuit' McVitie